I wonder if I might have something of yours to hold?" Madame Karitska said to the girl. "Something that you wear every day. A watch, a necklace, a ring."

"I wear this ring every day," the girl said, and slipped it from her finger and across the ornate coffee table.

Madame Karitska picked up the ring and was silent, holding it in the palm of her hand and closing her eyes to avoid distractions. Almost at once she jumped. Opening her eyes, she said in astonishment, "But this is the ring of a woman who died by violence—by murder."

She stared at the girl. "You are in great danger," she said. "Great danger."

Madame Karitska knew more than she was telling. But she did not know that within a few short days she would become embroiled in a brutal and puzzling case of murder.

The Clairvoyant Countess

Dorothy Gilman

A FAWCETT CREST BOOK

Fawcett Publications, Inc., Greenwich, Connecticut

For Bob and Barb Spence especially, and for psychics Ida Harrington and Vivian Meyer

THE CLAIRVOYANT COUNTESS

THIS BOOK CONTAINS THE COMPLETE TEXT OF THE ORIGINAL HARDCOVER EDITION.

A Fawcett Crest Book reprinted by arrangement with Doubleday & Company, Inc.

ISBN 0-449-22965-3

Printed in Canada

Chapter 1

The sign in the window of the shabby brownstone building said simply *Madame Karitska, Readings*.

Actually Marina Karitska was a countess but this was of small regard to her and certainly she had never been a run-of-the-mill countess. She was first of all clairvoyant and, secondly, she had spent her childhood years in the Far East as a beggar; it had been her first occupation. During the intervening years she had become fabulously rich in Budapest, had lost her wealth in Antwerp, and was extremely poor in America but she had a saying, born of experience, that only the eternal things mattered.

Among clairvoyants it is common knowledge that to use such a gift for personal profit is to invite loss of the sixth sense. In all the years of her eventful life Madame Karitska had never accepted money for her readings, but some months ago—eking out a living as a milliner in Trafton—she had begun to have a series of dreams, all of them alike night after night. In these dreams she was walking along a street that was foreign to her, and inevitably she would come to a particular brownstone house and observe in the first-floor window a sign that read *Madame Karitska, Readings.* The brownstone was one of many on a shabby street, indistinguishable from the others except for the fact that its front door was painted a bright canary yellow.

After experiencing this dream for a number of consecutive nights Madame Karitska found herself—seemingly by chance—going out of her way on a Sunday stroll. And suddenly she discovered herself standing and staring at a particular brownstone house in a long row of such houses, all of them identical except that this one had a bright yellow door. In the window to the left of the door hung a sign: APARTMENT FOR RENT.

Because this sort of thing had happened to her a few times before in her life Madame Karitska knew that her life was about to change again. She walked up the steps and tugged at an old-fashioned push-bell. A young man with a beard and a ring in one ear answered her summons. There were daubs of yellow and green paint across his jeans, and a freckle of alizarin crimson on the bridge of his nose. He was clearly astonished. "I only hung that sign in the window five minutes ago," he told her accusingly.

"Yes," she said. "May I see the apartment?"

There were two rooms, quite small but filled with light and ample enough for her hundreds of books, and there was a closet of a kitchen as well. It could all be rented for a sum less than what she paid for one room in the mediocre hotel in which she stayed.

"Of course the neighborhood's pretty lousy," the young man told her, for Marina Karitska continued to look like a countess through all the exigencies of life.

"In what way?" she asked with interest.

"It's a slum," he pointed out. "Mostly artists' lofts and lodgings."

"But quite safe for clients?"

"Clients?" he said in a startled voice.

"I shall be giving readings."

He looked relieved. "Oh—Christian Science. Yeah, the neighborhood's safe enough. The police station's just around the corner, you know. Down at the west end there's a lot of junkies but that's six blocks away. It's a straight neighborhood, just poor."

"Good—so am I," she told him crisply, and moved in two days later.

"And now we shall see," mused Madame Karitska when she had abandoned her milliner's job, scavenged lumber for bookcases, and unpacked her books. Her purse was flat but her serenity untouched. She had, after all, been much poorer in earlier days. Her parents had fled Russia when she was an infant, and since they did not know a great deal about money, having always had a vast amount of it, their silver lasted them only until they reached a wretched little town in the Urals where they were forced rather abruptly to learn what a deficiency of the commodity meant. Those members of the family who could work worked for a pittance. Those who could not begged. A title was useless but brains were not. By the time she was ten Marina Karitska had discovered a way to make paper flowers to sell in the bazaars at feast days, and by doing this she accumulated enough profit to move her family to Kabul, where they prospered and she became a student. In the years since then she had lost two husbands and a considerable fortune to wars and politics but she considered it merely the rounding of a circle. Poverty of circumstance did not imply impoverishment of spirit; by applying herself to life with diligence and scholarliness something would inevitably turn up.

What turned up on Eighth Street was at first not encouraging: she met rather too many foolish, lovesick women who saw her sign in the window and assumed her to be a common fortuneteller. But lately there had begun to be a few appointments by telephone, and serious ones, so that she began to feel that news of her existence was spreading beyond the neighborhood.

On this particular morning Madame Karitska had a nine-o'clock appointment that had been made by telephone the evening before. She was up at sunrise to meditate, after which she performed various yoga exercises, dressed, and had a meager breakfast. The knock on her door came promptly at nine.

"Good morning," she said, throwing open her door, and was at once enchanted by the prim, lovely young girl on her doorstep. "Come in, won't you? Do you like Turkish coffee or American? I've a pot of each on the stove."

The girl was plainly nervous but she brightened at Madame Karitska's warm welcome. "American, please."

No sense of adventure here, thought Madame Karitska; a pity. "Sit down, won't you?" she called, going to the tiny kitchen. "Preferably by the coffee table where I shall place the cups."

A moment later she was back, bearing a tray with carafe and cups. As the girl busied herself with sugar and milk, Madame Karitska frankly observed her. Beautiful but inhibited, she thought; frightened, but possibly of me. Very lonely. An odd young woman, odd because in spite of her beauty she had no awareness of its effect. Possibly men frightened her, possibly life itself. She would have to be very gentle with her. She said firmly, "I wonder if I might have something of yours to hold, I find it an excellent way to get acquainted. Something that you wear every day. A watch, a necklace, a ring."

The girl looked at her and Madame Karitska thought that if she were not so inhibited she would laugh. "What does that do?" the girl asked very politely.

"It is a matter of vibrations and tone," explained Madame Karitska forgivingly. "Whatever you wear takes on the emotional tone of both your body and your thoughts. It's called psychometry. I'm not a fortuneteller," she added firmly, "I'm a psychic."

The authority in her voice had its effect. "I wear this ring every day," the girl said, and slipped it from her finger and across the ornate coffee table.

"Thank you. Incidentally is there anything in particular that you want to know?"

The girl moved one hand in a curiously helpless gesture. "Oh, almost anything, I guess. Whether I should change jobs, for instance—"

Madame Karitska gave her a quick, shrewd glance. She had a strong feeling that the young woman suffered more from a general dissatisfaction with her life than from anything so specific as a job. Unlock her and she would begin living, she thought, but something was seriously blocking her.

Madame Karitska picked up the ring and was silent, holding it in the palm of her hand and closing her eyes to avoid distractions. Almost at once she jumped. Opening her eyes she said in astonishment. "But this is the ring of a woman who died by violence—by murder."

The young girl looked at her blankly.

"I get a vivid picture of a woman. A very happy woman in her late forties, I think, newly married—a second marriage, I feel. She has blond hair worn in—yes, in a sort of coronet. A braid wrapped around the head."

The girl's eyes widened. "But you're describing my mother."

"The ring is hers?"

"It was until a year ago."

"She is alive still?"

The girl shook her head. "No, she died thirteen months ago. Of a heart attack," she added dryly, "and in her sleep."

Madame Karitska did not comment. She handed back the ring. "I think we had better use something entirely your own. Frequently the impressions left by a former owner remain far stronger than those that follow. Have you something that has never belonged to anyone else?"

The girl's laugh was harsh. "I hope you do better with me than with my mother." She opened her purse. "I left my wrist watch at the apartment. What sort of thing can I give you instead—my wallet?"

"That will do," said Madame Karitska, and accepted a worn alligator wallet. "You've not finished your coffee," she said gently. "Let me concentrate a moment on this." After a pause she said, "You grew up—I see the state of Massachusetts, is this not right? A gray house with white shutters and a sundial in the back yard . . . A very old sundial set on a cement foundation."

The girl's eyes widened. "That's true."

Madame Karitska's eyes had turned remote. "And you are—" She stopped as she felt a chill run down her spine. "Is there a letter in this wallet?" she asked. "Or something—a memo—written by another person?"

The girl said in an astonished voice, "Why, yes, there's a letter. I keep it there."

Madame Karitska looked at the girl. She said quietly, "I don't know who the letter is from but I must tell you not to trust the person who wrote it." She felt suddenly very alarmed. "You are surrounded by violence, do you know that? Have you been aware of it?"

The girl had gone white. She said in a primly angry voice, "I think you're quite mad. That letter is from a very dear person, the only person left in the whole world whom I trust. How dare you say he's not to be trusted!"

Madame Karitska looked deeply into her eyes. She said softly, "If you continue to believe this then you may find yourself in a difficult situation. I get a picture of a person whose charm—and there is great charm—conceals very disturbed emotions. This person is motivated by a deeply destructive—"

The girl put down her coffee cup and stood up. She

said angrily, "You don't know what you're talking about, I'm sorry I ever came, I—"

"But you did come," pointed out Madame Karitska calmly.

The girl turned scarlet.

"You came," said Madame Karitska, "because at some level deep within you there is awareness of something very wrong. Think about this, it is all I ask of you, for why should my words disturb you if you are so very certain I am in error? No, no, I will not accept money, this has been uncomfortable for me as well. You think I like to upset people?"

"You've not upset me at all," the girl said furiously, and picked up her purse.

Madame Karitska reached out and caught the girl's free hand. She turned it, palm up, and glanced at it, then holding it quivering for a moment in hers she said very gently, "You do not know me, I do not know you, is this not right? What could I want from you? What have I taken from you except a few minutes of your time? Consider me only a stranger who warns you—even a fool—but allow yourself to think carefully." She released her hand and stood up. "If you do not," she said, "grave harm may come to you. You trust too easily."

The girl looked at her, started to say something, and then flung herself instead toward the door. Opening it she said over her shoulder in a choked voice, "One of the girls at the office said you were great—just great." She was like a child who has been cheated as she said, *"Good-by!"*

When the door had closed behind her Madame

Karitska stood silent, her eyes thoughtful, and then with a sigh she picked up the empty cups and carried them into the kitchen.

Chapter 2

When Detective-Lieutenant Pruden arrived at the apartment the lab man and the police photographer were already there. "Thought you'd never get here," said Sergeant Swope. "We've begun fingerprints. Could you tell me inside of four minutes if you want anything else?"

"You running late too?" Pruden murmured absently, his eyes moving over the scene. He was a compact, well-put-together man with fair hair and tilted, skeptical, thick brows over slate-blue eyes. He detached himself from Swope and walked across the room to the body of the girl that lay sprawled across the couch, her dead eyes staring ceilingward. This was a bloody one, a *very* bloody one he realized as he stepped over the pool of blood beside the couch. The knife still lay on the floor, a long butcher's knife red to the hilt. With it the girl had been stabbed in the chest at least half a dozen times.

"No prints on the knife," Swope said, following him. "Wiped clean. Not even a bloody footprint on the rug."

"Smart killer."

"Good-looking gal."

Pruden was only too aware of this: slender, blond, a neat little figure in bell-bottom slacks and a turtleneck sweater. He leaned over and touched her and was surprised. "It happened around midnight, then?"

"That's Doc's estimate. Between eleven and 1 A.M."

"She live alone?"

Swope nodded. "The clock-radio'd been set for 6:30 A.M., and loud, very loud. Apparently like a siren. The neighbors on both sides came over and knocked and shouted, and still it kept ringing, and there was no answer to their knock, so they called the super and he went in with his key."

"Interesting," said Pruden, his glance falling on the face of the girl on the couch. "She doesn't look to me as if anything in her life was too loud. Soft gray sweater, soft gray slacks, all the colors in the room pale, as if she went through life on tip-toe." He called to the fingerprint man, "Charlie, dust the clock-radio, front, back, sides, and knobs. Okay, how did her assailant get in?"

"The front door was locked. The super's absolutely positive about this. It has to have been the fire escape at the kitchen window."

"Show me," said Pruden, and they walked across the small living room to the tiny box of a room beyond it. There was a large window with a drop-leaf table in front of it. The window lacked bars but held a screen that hooked on the inside; it was unhooked now. "It was like this when you arrived?"

"Yes. Ogilvy's already taken pictures of it."

He called, "Charlie? Make sure you dust this window out here for prints, inside and outside; he may have gotten careless on the fire-escape side." He leaned over and examined a smudge of red on the soiled white sill. "Get me a close-up of this, too," he added, "and then have one of the lab boys dig it out and run a test on it." His eyes ran over the kitchen: everything clean and tidy, no unwashed dishes or glasses. "All right," he said, "tell me about her, give me a run-down. Name?"

"Alison Bartlett, age twenty-one. Lived in this apartment eleven months. Secretary. Quiet. Kept to herself. Landlord says he's never been aware of visitors here."

"Where did she work?"

"According to the papers at her desk, at Ebbets Publishing. I checked it out on the super's phone, and an Alison Bartlett has worked there for eleven months, first as typist, then as secretary. That's all I got from a routine call to personnel. Her boss's name is Stevenson."

"Good enough." He walked over to the couch and stared down at the girl. "Funny," he said, frowning, "she doesn't look terrified, she looks astonished."

Swope nodded. "It hits them that way sometimes. Fast. Too fast to register."

Pruden nodded. "She can be moved now. They get a picture of that desk over there?" When Swope replied in the affirmative he approached it with interest. It was a small student desk with a typewriter stand at right angles to it, and a stack of good bond paper beside it, all of it inscribed with the name of Ebbets Publishing Company. The two drawers he pulled open showed nothing of particular interest: writing paper, canceled checks, colored pencils, four six-by-eight reproductions of Van Gogh paintings, a paperback Bartlett's Quotations, one earring, a swizzle stick, a guidebook to the city. All of these would be examined later, slowly and patiently. The top of the desk was more communicative: there were bills and an engagement calendar with loose-leaf pages.

He turned the pages of the latter curiously, noting the number of empty pages. Those carrying inscriptions were meager: lunch with Ginny, a hairdresser appointment, reminder of a book due at the library, lunch with Ethel, hairdresser appointment . . . this seemed to be the shape of Alison Bartlett's life: neat, organized, and empty. Ten days ago, however, she had jotted down the words "Ask for tomorrow off," and with interest he turned the page. This time the sheet held a name and an address: Karitska, 11 Eighth Street.

It was something, anyway. He copied the address into his memo pad and tucked it away in his pocket. The phone rang and Swope wrapped a handkerchief around the receiver before plucking it from the cradle. He said, "The super says there are three news reporters waiting downstairs. Impatiently."

"They're going to love this one," Pruden said dryly.

"You can say that again." Swope's voice was savage. "It'll scare the daylights out of every young girl living alone in Trafton. Killer loose. Mad killer?"

"That," said Pruden, "is up to us to find out." He turned and looked again at the small dead face as the body was placed on the stretcher. In death it was almost but not quite nondescript. He wondered what the sterile pages of that engagement calendar concealed: an affair, blackmail, drugs, abortionists, or just one more lonely victim of the big city? He knew that before the case was finished he would come to know Alison Bartlett better than her friends and even her parents had known her.

It was midafternoon before Pruden zeroed in on the notation in the engagement calendar. Swope was still at work canvassing the neighborhood to find anyone who might have seen the murderer on the fire escape, or suspicious strangers entering the building. So far nothing had turned up. The afternoon paper was on the street, carrying Alison Bartlett's high-school graduation picture on its front page, and a headline that read GIRL BUTCHERED IN APARTMENT. By this time Pruden knew a little more about Alison Bartlett but not as much as he'd expected. One of the few things he did know, however, was that she didn't belong on Eighth Street, and he was curious. It was a cloudy, oppressive afternoon, and the brief thunderstorm at noon had accomplished nothing for the neighborhood except to blow over a few garbage pails, which did not improve the appearance of a block that hovered precariously on the edge of being a slum. Number 11 had a bright yellow door; to the left of the door, on the first floor, hung a sign: *Madame Karitska, Readings*.

What the hell—*readings?* thought Pruden, and rang the bell. When no one answered he opened the unlocked front door, walked into the hall, and knocked on the first door to the left. He thought this added a new dimension to Alison Bartlett; her coming here was the first untidy note that appeared to have entered her immaculate life.

The door opened, and Pruden found himself surprised. The woman facing him was tall, in her midforties, and dressed in a well-cut tweed pants suit. Good bones, was his first clinical impression; dark hair parted in the center, pulled severely back into a knot, and a face strong enough to survive the severity. Her eyes were striking, deeply set and lidded but oddly penetrating. A passionate face, he decided, and an unusual one. He rather enjoyed the unusual. He decided that she didn't belong on Eighth Street either.

"Come in, won't you?" said Madame Karitska, and turned her back on him to lead him inside.

The room he entered seemed flooded with light after the dark hallway. It contained almost exclusively books set in bookcases that occupied every inch of wall space. Arranged in the center of the room, however, was a couch, a low, intricately carved table in front of it, and a chair. He said grimly, "If you read the newspapers you ought to know you shouldn't allow strangers inside so casually."

She turned and looked at him with interest. "But I don't feel that we're strangers at all. Sit down, won't you? I've no appointments for an hour, and I've coffee in the kitchen. Would you prefer Turkish or American?"

For some reason Pruden said, "Turkish. What kind of appointments?"

She emerged from the other room, bearing tiny cups on a tray, and without reply poured an almost lava-like substance into the cups. "I'm delighted that you prefer Turkish," she said. "It's my one luxury in America. So many people find the grains abrasive and the brew too strong for them."

Pruden took a sip of Turkish coffee, shuddered, but withheld comment.

"But I think," she added with a faint smile, "that you have come for a more specific purpose than to ask what I mean by appointments."

"Yes." He removed the small photo of Alison Bartlett from his pocket and watched her closely as he handed the slip of cardboard across the table to her. She looked at it and a flash of something resembling pain crossed her features. Handing it back she said, "Yes, I recall her very well."

"Recall her?"

"She came here about ten days ago. By appointment but without giving a name."

"Of course you've read about her in the newspaper," he said.

"On the contrary, I do not read newspapers," she said firmly, "but I would guess that you are from the police."

"Then it's a bit difficult to believe that you don't read newspapers."

She shrugged. "Many people come here, I don't have to read newspapers. The outside world has no interest for me, only the inner worlds. Out there"—she waved a hand—"out there is only negativeness, violence, confusion, hostility—"

"That's why police are necessary," he said dryly. "Now tell me about Alison Bartlett."

"This girl?"

"Yes, what did she come here for? What did she want? You're some kind of fortuneteller?"

Madame Karitska surveyed him steadily from beneath her curiously hooded lids. "I'm a psychic, Mr.—?"

"Lieutenant Pruden."

"She did not know why she came here," went on Madame Karitska, "and the advice I gave her she could not accept. She is dead by violence?"

Pruden barely concealed a derisive smile. "Then of course you read the newspapers. Yes, she's been murdered. Some psycho broke into her apartment last night and killed her with a butcher's knife."

Madame Karitska shook her head. "You are quite wrong."

"I beg your pardon?"

Madame Karitska nodded, ignoring the dangerous tilt of his eyebrows. "I said you are quite wrong. On the contrary, you will eventually discover she was not killed by a stranger. I will tell you this: the clue to her murder lies in the death of her mother some months ago. Presumably the mother died of natural causes—a heart attack, the girl said—but in truth she was murdered. I saw it clearly—a vivid picture. Her mother was poisoned."

Pruden did not know whether to explode into anger or to laugh; in the end he only concealed a smile and said politely, "I see."

Madame Karitska's smile was open and very charming. "You need not believe me, Lieutenant Pruden; it is of no consequence to me whether you do or not, but you will not find your murderer among the violent ones in this city, I assure you. Did you find a letter in Miss Bartlett's wallet?"

He stared at her. "No."

"Then it had been removed. But find the letter that she carried folded in her wallet, a letter from someone she trusted and adored, and you will find her murderer."

"She showed you this letter?"

Madame Karitska gestured impatiently. "Of course not, but I could feel its emanations: they were terrible, ugly, vindictive, warped."

Pruden sighed, crossed his legs and decided to try a different tack. "Perhaps you would describe for me everything the girl said?"

"Of course," said Madame Karitska cheerfully, "but it was very little—I disappointed her and she did not remain. I'll try to think——" She put both hands to her temples and slowly recreated her few moments with the girl, describing the visit in detail.

"This picture you claim comes to your mind," said the lieutenant, curious in spite of himself.

"I never explain it to skeptics," she said firmly. "I will say only that it is a sixth sense, a gift for sensing what is invisible to others, for seeing what *is* and has been. In this case I was holding a ring which had belonged to the girl's mother. She was undoubtedly wearing it when she died."

Pruden nodded. "Very interesting," he said, and put down his cup of Turkish coffee.

"You've not finished it," said Madame Karitska with an amused smile.

Pruden found himself smiling back at her, and then —suddenly uneasy at what she might guess of his thoughts, for there *was* something uncanny about her—

he frowned. "I've got to be going. I won't say I swallow any more of this than I did of your coffee but it's interesting. Something they never mentioned in Police College," he added wryly.

"A pity," she said. "I understand the Russians are devoting whole college courses to psychic phenomena, but of course Americans continue to resist it." She sighed and stood up to usher him to the door. "Oh by the way, Lieutenant Pruden," she said as he reached the door.

"Yes?"

"Your father is in the hospital and not expected to live, is this not correct? I think you will find the doctors are quite wrong and that he will begin to mend by the weekend."

Pruden looked hard and long at her and then flung open the door and went out.

Alison Bartlett's body was claimed by her stepfather the next day, and Pruden met him at the morgue, where the man introduced himself as Carl Madison. He looked distraught, his eyes red-rimmed, his tie askew. He was guilt-stricken, he said; he had taken great pains not to interfere with Alison's desire to be independent after her mother's death and now this had happened; he should never have allowed her to come to the city. Pruden murmured the usual, asked a few questions about Alison's life in Massachusetts, the body was signed over to Madison, and he left on his sad journey home.

A week later the public murmurings over the Bartlett murder had grown into an uproar and Pruden and Swope had learned nothing more than they'd known twenty-four hours after the girl's death. Every possible lead had been followed to its source, every molester, loiterer, pimp, and known psychotic in their files checked out and still there was nothing. A big fat cipher. The county prosecutor was beginning to make angry statements. He was threatening his own investigation, and that, as Pruden's superior grimly pointed out, threw a very bad light on the efficiency of the department.

Pruden said, "I'd like to go to Massachusetts and poke around for a few days."

"She wasn't murdered in Massachusetts," pointed out the Chief. "She was murdered here in Trafton."

Pruden hesitated, a little embarrassed. "Look," he said uneasily, "there's always the chance we've gone about this wrong, isn't there? I know McGill checked Massachusetts but it was only an inquiry to see if the girl had any rejected boy friends or had mentioned any men she met in Trafton. I think there could be more to it than that." He said doggedly, "I'm thinking of the questions we ask in premeditated murders, like who benefits from a person's death, that sort of thing."

The Chief sighed. "You're grasping at straws, Pruden. This was no premeditated murder, it was a crazy, insane, violent act. A dope addict, a psycho—"

"Maybe that's what we're supposed to think," Pruden said stubbornly.

"Pruden, 99 per cent of murders in the city are stupid, spur-of-the-moment, unpremeditated, insane acts of rage. Don't complicate things for yourself."

"There was no look of terror on her face," pointed out Pruden. "I keep remembering that. There was only astonishment. A girl like that, finding a strange person in her apartment in the middle of the night and seeing him with a butcher's knife—"

"She didn't see it coming," pointed out the Chief. "It's happened before. The killer assures her he's only after her radio, her cash, etcetera. A nice girl like that believes him, feels maternal about him, a little helpful, and then—pow. There isn't time for terror, only astonishment."

Pruden sighed. "All right, then let me put it this way. There's one tip I've never investigated."

The Chief's jaw dropped. "You're kidding. Who from? What is it?"

Pruden winced. "I'd rather not say, at least until I've checked it out. It's too far out—way out. In fact if I told you, you'd laugh your head off. But we've found nothing and I figure even the wildest tip is worth looking into at this point."

The Chief considered, his eyes on Pruden's face. "All right," he said slowly, his eyes narrowing. "I've no desire to laugh in your face, not when I can see the day coming when the county prosecutor laughs in mine. I don't know what I can tell the press while you're gone but Swope can take over for the moment. How much time do you need?"

Pruden reflected. "I haven't seen the papers, the funeral was held in midweek?"

The Chief nodded. "In Massachusetts. Full coverage by the press."

"Do you know who her lawyer is?"

The Chief shook his head. "No, but it's a small town, population eight hundred and fifty, and she lived there all her life. There'll be her friends, teachers, minister, stepfather."

Pruden nodded. "I'll leave this afternoon."

"Oh by the way," said the Chief as Pruden reached the door, "anything new on your father?"

Pruden's face brightened but his voice, when he spoke, was singularly dry. "Quite a bit, actually. Over the weekend he came out of his coma and they believe he's going to pull through now."

Chapter 3

It was strange, Pruden thought, how strikingly different Alison Bartlett's murder seemed from this end of the telescope, this sleepy New England village, population 858. A light snow was falling, one of those perverse spring flurries that happen in April in the North. He stopped first at the bank and inquired the name of the family's lawyer; it seemed reasonable to suppose they would have one.

"They opened Alison's safe-deposit box just this morning," the manager said. "The will goes into probate now. Tragedy," he added with a shake of his head. "You'll find Eben Johnson across the street. Second floor, the white clapboard building."

He walked up creaking wooden stairs and entered a door marked Johnson & Taggart, Attorneys-at-Law. It was a pleasant, cluttered, shabby office; a cheerful teenager with long blond hair waved him to a seat, poked her head into the adjoining office, and then said he could go in.

"Eben Johnson?" he said to the man behind the desk, and holding out his hand added, "Lieutenant Pruden, detective division of the Trafton police."

Johnson stood and reached across the desk to shake his hand. He was a man who had seen his most active days. He looked frail, his skull showing under thin gray hair, mouth pursed, his eyes warm and kind. "You must be here about Alison," he said, and an expression of sadness crossed his face. "A tragedy-stalked family, a terrible shock to us all. Sit down, won't you?"

"Gladly," said Pruden.

"Ruthie," he called, lifting his voice, "bring us coffee." He sat back and looked at Pruden. "I've known Alison all her life and I never thought—it's shaken this town, shaken our beliefs, our smugness, our—" He stopped and shook his head. "Suppose *you* tell *me.*"

Pruden considered a moment and decided the contents of any will or safe-deposit box could wait. "I want to know, not about Alison, but about her mother."

"Her *mother!*" exclaimed Johnson, and looked not only taken aback but alarmed. "Alison's mother," he repeated as Ruthie walked in bearing a tray with two cups of coffee on it. "Thanks," he said absently, and as the girl headed out he called, "Close the door behind you, will you, Ruthie?"

Pruden sat still, wary and alert. "I startled you?"

The man hesitated. "Yes." He held out one of the cups to Pruden. "Sugar? Cream?"

"Just sugar. Why have I startled you?"

He shook his head. "It's difficult to say. Francine—Alison's mother—has been very much on my mind this week, somehow, and you walked into this office and seemed to read my mind. She's dead, you know. Died over a year ago. March 7," he added.

Pruden sipped his coffee, eyes on the man. "Heart attack, I understand?"

"Yes." His voice was short.

"You're not sure?"

Johnson looked down at his coffee. "Of course I'm sure. Of course I'm sure," he repeated slowly. "It's just—"

Pruden said softly, "If you'd talk it out, no matter how whimsical it might sound—"

Johnson's mouth curved in an ironic smile. "Lawyers are not whimsical, Lieutenant Pruden. As a lawyer, however, I've represented the Bartlett family for as many years as I've been practicing law. When Tom married Francine and they bought the old Whittaker house I handled the closing and the title search. I drew up Tom's will, just as I'd drawn up his father's, and I amended it for him after Alison's birth. When Tom was killed in a car crash in '60 I handled the estate, or what was left of it, and drew up a new will for Francine after she was a widow."

"I met her second husband in Trafton early this week."

"Yes, she married again. . . . Let's say I could never reconcile myself to Francine's death because I could never reconcile myself to her second marriage."

"I see," murmured Pruden, recalling the stocky, good-looking, distraught man he'd encountered at the morgue. "Why?"

The old man shrugged. "I'm seventy-six, Lieutenant Pruden, and I'm a Victorian and I have my prejudices. I don't like to see a man living off his wife's money. In my day Carl Madison would have been called a kept man."

"But I thought you said there was very little money when Tom Bartlett was killed."

"That's right, he didn't leave much except debts, which Francine paid off slowly, year by year, after she was appointed town librarian. But Tom's aunt died several years later and Francine came into quite a bit of money."

"Money!" exclaimed Pruden, and put down his cup hard.

Johnson nodded. 'When the estate taxes had been paid it amounted to three hundred thousand dollars, and that," he said dryly, "is a fortune in my book. That's when Francine celebrated by taking herself and Alison on a Caribbean cruise."

"She met her second husband there, this Carl Madison?" Pruden said sharply.

Johnson nodded. "She came home married, looking radiant, enchanted, like a child. Alison adored the man too." He shrugged. "Pleasant-enough fellow, except—"

"Yes?"

Johnson stirred uneasily. "Except he's lived in this town for seven years now and I don't think anybody knows him any better than they did when they first met him. Keeps to himself out there in the Whittaker house, and kept Francine and Alison to himself too. The marriage changed Francine; we hardly ever saw her. Just the three of them, like recluses."

"All right," Pruden said harshly, "who got Francine's money when she died?"

Johnson lifted his eyes and looked thoughtfully at Pruden. "Alison received the majority of it. Carl Madison was left the house and fifty thousand dollars."

"And Alison's will? There *is* a will?"

"Indeed yes," said Johnson dryly. "I drew it up for her just before she left for Trafton. She leaves everything to her stepfather."

Pruden was silent, a strange excitement stirring in him. "What was Alison's relationship to her stepfather?"

"Positively incestuous, I'd say. After Francine's death Alison insisted he lack for nothing. You could almost say she was brokenhearted that Francine had left her husband so little and herself so much."

"Why did she go to Trafton, then, if she was so close to him?"

Johnson hesitated and then he said slowly, "I had the feeling that she just might be in love with her stepfather."

"Then I don't understand why she left."

Johnson nodded. "It crossed my mind, at the time, that they might marry. Perhaps I was being cynical but Madison had become accustomed to living well and here was this eager, charming young girl with a quarter of a million dollars caring about him." He shook his head. "But Alison had a puritanical streak in her, and I think that's why she chose to—just leave. I don't think she was able to cope with being in love with her mother's husband."

"How did Madison take it, being left only the house and a small share of the money?"

"Not well," Johnson said dryly. "Not well at all, a fact that I took pains not to communicate to Alison. Perhaps I should have, but I've seen much saintlier men fall apart over money."

"Mr. Johnson," said Pruden, "what are your suspicions about Francine Bartlett's death?"

Johnson looked startled. "Suspicions? On the contrary," he said, "I didn't realize I had any until you walked in and asked." He hesitated. "But they've been there. I have to confess I've always felt—uneasy, unsettled—about her death. You see, I did a very untypical thing after meeting Carl Madison for the first time."

"Yes?"

The old man looked uncomfortable. "I tried making inquiries about him. I felt—skeptical, unsatisfied. I wasn't happy about what I did, and later I decided I was a damn fool, but you have to understand that I looked on Francine almost as a daughter. She was a lovely person, left widowed at a ridiculous age. She was young, delightful, courageous. The town protected her, she was one of ours, at least until she married Madison."

"Yet you did make inquiries. What did you discover?"

"Nothing," he said simply. "Nothing at all. The Illinois town where he said he was born had no records of his birth. He'd been a chemist, he said—no way to trace that—and had gone to Syracuse University. They hadn't heard of him either. I finally decided to let sleeping dogs lie."

"Did you remember all this when Francine died?"

Johnson sighed. "I suppose it crossed my mind, but

we're not accustomed to melodrama here in Pennsville, Lieutenant; and then you see Francine *did* have asthma. Rather badly, poor child. In fact it's hard to picture or describe Francine without the little aerosol vial she always carried with her in case of attacks. It was like a reflex with her, absently bringing it out to sniff the way others light a cigarette."

Pruden's eyes narrowed. "And you say he was a *chemist?*"

Johnson looked at him questioningly. "Yes, it's what he said he was seven years ago."

Pruden stood up. "Mr. Johnson, do you know where or how I could get a photograph of Carl Madison?"

Johnson looked startled and then thoughtful. He said, "I don't think Francine would mind." He rose and walked stiffly to a file cabinet in the corner and drew out a small glossy photograph. "Francine gave me this, it's a shipboard photograph taken at their wedding on the way home. I don't think Carl Madison ever knew she gave it to me, so I've tactfully kept it tucked away." He handed over the picture.

Pruden looked at the three people in the photograph: they made a handsome portrait of a sun-tanned, carefree family. He said, "Do you mind if I borrow this for a few days? I'll have copies made and return it to you."

Johnson looked vaguely unhappy. "Look, you understand emotions get involved here. I hope I've not implied, not suggested—I'm a churchgoing man, Lieutenant."

Pruden told him gently, "On the contrary, you've suggested nothing that hadn't already been suggested to me, and I can't tell you how helpful you've been."

"Certainly not in helping you solve Alison's brutal murder!"

"That," said Pruden, buttoning up his trench coat, "is for me to find out."

Chapter 4

It was nine o'clock and Madame Karitska threw open the shutters of her living room to inhale the morning air with delight. "A gorgeous day!" she exclaimed.

Behind her Kristan said, "You can't pay your rent and it's a gorgeous day?"

"Give me a few hours," she said, turning to him. "I promise I shall have it—I feel it."

Her young landlord considered this a moment, his bearded face troubled. "You understand I am at this minute so poor myself I couldn't pay rent if I hadn't leased the building. As an artist—"

She nodded. "But of course, I would not for the world ask you to wait for money that belongs to you. If something does not turn up I shall sell my last diamond for you."

"*Diamond?*"

She shrugged. "Yes, my second husband was a diamond merchant in Antwerp and I have managed to keep a few. Now only one is left, small but very fine. It is my security."

"Well, that's a relief," her young landlord said doubtfully, "because I'd hate to see you go. Hey, your phone's ringing, Madame Karitska."

She smiled magnificently. "Yes it is, isn't that miraculous? In spite of the bill being unpaid?"

She answered the telephone in a confident voice. The woman on the other end of the line was apologetic and pleading. A charity tea at her town house was taking place that afternoon, in her garden, and would it be possible for Madame Karitska to replace the fortune-teller they'd hired to amuse the guests? Her niece, an art student, had visited Madame Karitska several weeks earlier and had said fine things about her. She would happily pay Madame Karitska seventy-five dollars for her two hours of work, and possibly there might be some tips.

Madame Karitska pretended to consult her engagement calendar. "But yes," she said with surprise and delight, "yes, I am free for those hours. How fortunate for us both!"

The woman gave the address, which was in the very elegant Cavendish Square area, and Madame Karitska promised to be there at two o'clock.

Her young landlord looked at her curiously. "You look like a cat that's just swallowed a canary," he told her.

"I am to be fortuneteller at a charity tea this afternoon. Seventy-five dollars!"

Kristan grinned. "Do you always get rescued like this?"

"Ah, my dear Kristan," she said lightly, "begin by living as if you had faith, and you will see!"

He said wryly, "I doubt if it would work for me, I swear too much."

"Then try swearing *less* much," she said tartly. "Now do go and let me begin my meditating, and if you hear anyone at my door between two and four tell them I shall be back!"

At fifteen minutes before the hour Madame Karitska presented herself at the magnificent brownstone house to which she had been directed. She was at first mistaken for a guest of Mrs. Faber-Jones but once this matter had been cleared up she was sent to the garden, upon which a great deal of time and money had been lavished. Two brownstone houses had been thrown together and remodeled with huge glass windows looking out upon the garden, which at this season was ablaze with colorful flowers and maze-like hedges. Small pink tents had been set up for refreshments and a yellow one for Madame Karitska; an orange marquee held a number of uniformed musicians who were to play chamber music, and small tables and gilt chairs had been placed among the shrubbery.

Madame Karitska had brought with her a flowing robe, which, in the absence of a crystal ball, Mrs. Faber-Jones agreed would be appropriate for her to wear. It was a pity, however, about no crystal ball, she said: the other woman would have brought one, but she had apparently been arrested by the police.

"There are many charlatans in the field," said Madame Karitska calmly, and took her place under several hanging flower baskets. "I am *not* one, however."

From the very beginning she felt that she was being watched closely but it was not until she had given several readings that she identified her attentive observer. He was a small, plump, middle-aged man, impeccably dressed, with ruddy skin and a somewhat whimsical white mustache. He looked rather like a very successful stockbroker or financier, and when he at last approached her during a lull, this was precisely what he turned out to be. He was John Faber-Jones, the husband of her hostess.

"I thought I'd ask a few questions," he said, "about —uh—what it's like to be a fortuneteller."

She would have thought this the last thing to interest him. "I'm not a fortuneteller, I'm a clairvoyant," she told him patiently.

"Ah, there's a difference, is there? You look so— well, so damned respectable, frankly."

He had been standing all the while with the sun behind him so that she could not see his face. Now she looked up, suddenly interested, and suggested he sit down in front of her and have a reading.

With an air of reluctance—almost of fear—he obeyed, and they faced each other, whereupon Madame Karitska began to smile. "I see," she said with amusement. "You are one of us!"

He looked startled and guilty. "It shows?"

"I can assure you I am the only one who would notice," she told him somewhat dryly.

He began to speak in halting, desperate sentences. He said that until three months ago he had been totally normal—totally, he emphasized grimly—but in February he had slipped on a patch of ice in front of his brokerage firm and had fallen unconscious to the ground. He had been taken to the hospital in an ambulance, and he had been unconscious for nearly twelve hours.

"That's when it happened," he said in a miserable voice.

"What—exactly?" she prodded gently.

"They had put me in a semiprivate room, opposite a hit-and-run victim," he explained in a low voice. "Soon after I became conscious I could hear and see them taking down notes on the accident this fellow had survived. They asked if there was any chance he'd noticed the license plate of the car that hit him. I looked across the room at this chap—he was sitting up, you know, not too badly hurt. I'd never seen him before in my life, and I—" His voice broke.

"Yes, do go on," said Madame Karitska.

"I made a damn fool of myself. I spoke up. I said the chap had been hit by a car with New York plates, license number YO 1836J1." He looked at her. "You can imagine the furor this caused. But, you see, the license plate was suspended over his head in a sort of cloud."

Madame Karitska nodded. "It happens," she said.

"I hope it doesn't happen often," he told her with a shiver. "And why it should happen to me—I can only tell you it's been absolute hell for me ever since. Oh, I can assure you I've not said a word about it, I've locked my lips. But since the accident—and that damn license number did turn out to belong to the car that hit that chap—I can't tell you what I've seen. It seems an absolutely filthy world!"

"Ah," said Madame Karitska, alerted.

"Yes." He looked really abject now. "I realize my wife despises me, and has for many years. My daughter is living in sin with a young hippie upstate, in some sort of commune, and one of my clerks is pilfering the accounts of the firm."

Madame Karitska concealed a smile. "Then you have just discovered what you have been surrounded by all your life. How fortunate! Perhaps you will be able to change some things. But this has tremendous meaning, you know."

"I keep hoping it will go away as suddenly as it came."

"Perhaps it will," she said cheerfully.

"All right, where does it come from?" he asked suddenly and angrily.

She laughed. "Oh my dear Mr. Faber-Jones, you wish the answer in one sentence? I can only tell you this: as human beings we remain very ignorant in spite of our splitting atoms and building vast machines. There is far more to the universe than we can possibly comprehend as yet, and there are laws of the universe that no scientists have as yet uncovered. To know ourselves may be the next frontier, because inside of each of us lies the clue to all time and space concepts, all—"

Abruptly she stopped, realizing that several people were waiting for her attention. Reaching out a hand she said consolingly, "Do not take it too severely, I beg of you. It can be heartbreaking, yes, and often it is terrifying, but for it to have happened in this manner —such a strange manner—is most challenging for you.

It was meant to happen, Mr. Faber-Jones. Trust it. Be patient, accept."

When Madame Karitska returned to her apartment it was with ninety-seven dollars in her purse, enough to pay her monthly rent and her telephone bill as well. She took it at once to the top floor where Kristan painted and lived.

"The rent?" he said in astonishment.

"The rent."

He counted it and tucked it away in his wallet. "Oh by the way, there's a Lieutenant Pruden waiting for you downstairs. I hope it's all right, but seeing he's a policeman I let him into your apartment."

Madame Karitska thanked him, avoided any second glance at his latest painting, which appeared to be a tangle of snakes placed on a bilious green background, and went downstairs. Opening the door to her apartment she found Pruden looking through the books in her bookcase. "So—we meet again," she said pleasantly.

He turned. "You certainly have a great many books on the occult here."

"As well as the Bible, the Koran, the Upanishads, the Dhammapada, and others," she pointed out lightly. "You look tired, Lieutenant."

He looked at her and she felt no hostility in his gaze today. He said simply, "I've been up all night reading books on ESP. I think we've found Alison Bartlett's murderer."

"Oh?"

"I know you don't read newspapers but—" He drew a folded paper from his pocket and handed it to her.

She unfolded it gingerly, as if it was distasteful to her, and read the leaping black headline: ARREST MADE IN ALISON'S MURDER; Stepfather arraigned. "Perhaps you will sit down and tell me about this," she said quietly.

"It was her stepfather. It took us days to prove that he'd ever left Massachusetts on April 2. Neighbors insisted his lights were on in the house all evening until midnight, but of course there are gadgets that turn lights on and off." At her puzzled frown he said, "His name is Carl Madison and he married Alison's mother seven years ago. Alison adored him."

"Ah," said Madame Karitska, comprehending.

"We had only a photograph—a blown-up photo—to work with. We figured that if he really was our chap he would have had to drive to New York, since buses or trains or planes would have been too conspicuous. He would have had to leave Massachusetts no later than 8 P.M. to reach Alison's apartment by midnight, knock on her door, enter, glance over escape possibilities, and then kill her. He would have been back in Massachusetts no later than 5 A.M., well in advance of any telephone call about her murder.

"We sneaked a look at the speedometer on his car and checked it out with the garage where his car was last serviced. Nothing there, but a knowledgeable amateur can set back a speedometer. We showed his photo to every tollbooth attendant outside of New York and batted zero. But two days ago we found an attendant in a Trafton parking lot who recognized Madison's face. One of those rare people who literally never forget a face. What's more, he remembered that Madison's license plates were daubed with mud, which was strange because it's been a dry season, and he had to do some scrubbing before he could note down the number for his records. The parking lot was about ten blocks from Alison's apartment. Apparently Madison was so terrified of his car being noticed by the police, or of getting ticketed for being parked on a street at that hour, that he made this one mistake. And so we were able to prove that he was in Trafton the night Alison was murdered."

Madame Karitska nodded. "Was that enough?"

"No," went on Pruden, "but it was enough to open things up." With a faint smile he added, "We then applied for permission to exhume the body of Alison's mother."

"Interesno," murmured Madame Karitska, with a lift of her brows.

"It made Madison nervous," said Pruden. "That man's a superb actor but it began the slow process of breaking down his confidence, and before the results of the lab tests were back we hit pay dirt on Madison's real identity. It turns out that he was born Norman Pãlos, and was an old hand at being a widower: he'd married twice before, each time to a young widow with money, and each time his wife had died of a heart attack in her sleep."

"Poison?" suggested Madame Karitska.

"It certainly was in Francine Bartlett's case. She'd inhaled it consistently for some months by way of a nose spray she used for asthma attacks. Madison had been a chemist; he doctored the vials. She may very well have died of a heart attack—it would weaken any heart to cope with increasing doses of arsenic—but there was enough poison still in her body to change the whole picture. At that point Madison cracked and confessed to murdering the two of them, which saved us a good bit of time."

"Yes," said Madame Karitska, and then, very simply, "I am glad he will not be allowed to do this again. He was a very evil man."

"You realize," Pruden said, looking at her squarely, "how much I'm indebted to you for this."

"I realize," she said imperturbably, "what you thought of my words when I spoke them several weeks ago to you in this room. You are more flexible than I supposed, Lieutenant."

"And very curious at this point," he admitted.

"I believe we were intended to meet," she told him with a faint smile, "and I am a little curious myself. Have you something on your person that you wear every day and have worn for some years?"

"You mean a reading?" he asked, and looked a little alarmed. "Well, I suppose—here, I'll give you my watch. A high-school graduation present worn for fifteen straight years."

"Very good," she murmured, and gave him a reassuring smile as he handed it to her. Closing her eyes she concentrated while Pruden watched her, half skeptical, half apprehensive. "Ah yes," she said at last, "I see how it is. My instincts were sound, we are not strangers to one another at all. I get an impression of a very fine brain, a most intelligent man."

"Of course," Pruden said flippantly.

"But," continued Madame Karitska, paying him no attention, "a rather inhibited man, a little narrow and literal. You have been too busy for love—a pity—but inside of fifteen months you will be married."

"That I refuse to believe," Pruden said, flushing.

"Believe it," Madame Karitska told him firmly. "She will have long pale hair—really *very* pale, so light in color it is very near to white, and she is—how interesting!" Madame Karitska opened her eyes and smiled at him. "She will have considerable clairvoyant ability, Lieutenant."

"Good Lord," he said mildly.

"But before you meet her you will have a very near brush with death," she went on, and her voice quickened. "Yes, yes, I see it, and it is very bad, you could be gravely harmed. There will be a Buddha-like figure, I cannot tell whether this is a living man or a statue. He wears reds and blues and he sits, and when you meet him you will be in terrible danger *from something unseen behind you*."

"Buddha?" he repeated skeptically. "It sounds rather exotic for my line of work."

She opened her eyes. "Then perhaps having been warned you will notice it more acutely," she said in a stern voice. "It looms like a shadow over your whole future, over the girl, over your becoming Commissar of Police."

"Over my becoming *what?*"

"Oh yes, you will go far," she assured him. "But you must take care, you understand?" She smiled. "One hopes so, for I look forward to getting further acquainted with you, Lieutenant. And now if you will forgive me," she said with a glance at her wrist watch, "I have an appointment in ten minutes."

Pruden rose and moved toward the door. As he reached it he heard a knock and, after a questioning glance at Madame Karitska, opened the door. A small boy stood there with a dirty, tear-stained face. *"This* is your appointment?" he asked, amused.

"He has lost his kitten," she told him calmly. "You must not think, Lieutenant, that the loss of a kitten is not also a cosmic event. We hope, between us, to discover where he may find it."

Chapter 5

Madame Karitska opened her door to Lieutenant Pruden one early morning several weeks later. "I came on impulse, without calling," he said. "Are you alone?" When she hesitated he rephrased this. "Can you be interrupted?"

She nodded. "Of course, Lieutenant."

He came in, looking around him. "I met your young landlord on the curb putting out the garbage, and he said you always act as if someone's with you, or shouldn't I mention the impression you've given him?"

"Consider it a small idiosyncrasy," said Madame Karitska with a smile. "What can I do for you?"

"As an opener you could tell me how in hell you look so cheerful mornings, and," he added with a grin, "if you're offering coffee I'll take Turkish."

"Marvelous, you will soon begin to appreciate it!"

Lighting a match under the carafe on the table she said, "I have the advantage over you of spending many years in the Far East and in eastern Europe as well. The reason for my sanguinity in the morning is both simple and complex: I have experienced much in the way of wise men and prophets." Carefully she poured Turkish brew into tiny cups. "If psychologists and sociologists claim that we went from the Age of Anxiety into the Age of Alienation, then the next era—for survival, I assure you—must be the Age of Consciousness."

He laughed. "If you're implying that none of us is conscious, Madame Karitska, I shall resent that very much."

She smiled at him. "Ah but actually, Lieutenant Pruden, almost every human being is totally sound asleep. We are sleep-walkers . . . Now what can I do for you, please?"

He removed a small plastic bag from his jacket, turned it upside down over the coffee table, and delivered a cascade of silver rings to its surface. There were perhaps a dozen of them, all alike. Madame Karitska picked up one and examined it: its design was one of a black enamel seal encircled by crimson with a motto in Latin. Inside the ring were the initials D.H.L. '78. She picked up another: its initials were G.A.M. '78.

"St. Bonaventure's School," contributed Lieutenant Pruden. "I've made half a dozen trips there and gotten nowhere. Let's see what a clairvoyant can do."

She gave him a sharp glance. "I'm not so sure I'm delighted to have met you! What precisely is the problem?"

"Petty thefts, but they add up and the school has a famous old reputation to preserve. These rings have been worn—presumably with pride—every day since January, when they were distributed among the freshman class upon their return from the holidays. You said you picked up—well, vibrations," he growled. "These rings belong to the students and one of them has to be the thief."

"A schoolboy thief," she mused. "But surely the police are well-equipped to uncover the culprit, and isn't there a school psychologist?"

"Yes to both," he said grimly. "But officially the police aren't in on it. My superior in the police department graduated from St. Bonaventure's and they've asked his help in avoiding any publicity. We've done what we could. We know it's one of these fourteen boys because the thefts occur only in Beecham Cottage, and always at night, when the dorm is locked securely.

"As for the school's psychologist," he continued, "he's examined the records of each of these fourteen boys and he can find none of them with any striking emotional problem or pattern that could lead to this sort of thing. The tests essential for admission are pretty thorough—Rorschach, Achievement, etcetera—and since these boys are freshmen the tests were all done within the last year. Running fresh tests on these boys would run into money and consume valuable school time. In the meanwhile the thefts continue—the ninth last night."

"What exactly has been stolen?" asked Madame Karitska curiously.

He handed her a small typed list. "It's getting to be a very bad business for St. Bonaventure's, this. The boys write home, the atmosphere's uneasy, the rumors growing. A number of parents have already called in, inquiring."

Madame Karitska was looking at the list.

> Rosary. Belonging to housemother. Antique. Amber. Value $175.
> Baseball glove, $15.
> Ivory cross, value $80.
> Silver cross, value $92.
> Hand-carved Tyrolean cross, about $15.
> Hand-carved chess set, Yugoslavian, $25.
> 2 Tennis racquets, $15. and $45.
> Prayer book, antique

"An interesting list," said Madame Karitska thoughtfully.

"A damn puzzling one. After every theft we've searched the dormitory—the last three times while the students were still there behind locked doors—and we found only two items."

"The tennis racquets," said Madame Karitska, nodding.

He gave her a sharp glance. "What made you guess that?"

"For one thing, they're the largest items. Have you searched the boys?"

Pruden shook his head. "This headmaster refuses—so far. I can't say I blame him. Parents of St. Bonaventure's boys don't shell out nearly four thousand dollars a year to see their sons stripped and searched like common criminals. On the other hand I've told Father Tuttle he may have to see it done if he wants this cleared up."

"And so you bring me the rings," said Madame Karitska musingly.

"Yes." He added wryly, "You know my skepticism. You understand my hopes."

She said with humor, "You are moving from disbelief to ambivalence. That is progress, no? I will call you. This will take a day at least."

"Right," he said, and with a sigh left an extremely comfortable chair to return to work.

Madame Karitska had three appointments that day. One of them surprised even her: she had reason to speak some very tough words to a spoiled, middle-aged woman who not only accepted them with good grace but left behind twenty-five dollars in the basket by the door. Between appointments Madame Karitska accomplished her chores with one or another of the fourteen rings on her fingers. She learned from the rings a great deal about St. Bonaventure's School and about the sort of boys who went there, as well as their grievances, affections, hatreds, and resentments, but by midnight she had learned nothing that would help Lieutenant Pruden.

"However," she told him at nine the next morning when she telephoned him, "there is one child there who is extremely disturbed about his family. I'm sorry that I can be of no help to you about the thefts but I pick up—I can only call them *tragic* emanations—from one of the rings. I want to talk to this boy if I may. The initials on his ring are"—she held up the ring to the light—"G.U.O."

"If it has nothing to do with the thefts," began Lieutenant Pruden.

She said crisply, "Please give me the name of this child."

Pruden sighed. She heard the crackling of paper; a list was apparently consulted and the lieutenant replied, "That would be Gavin Ulbright O'Connell, I daresay."

"Thank you. Shall I visit him at school, or would you suggest bringing him here to me?" She added gently, "I can only tell you, my dear Lieutenant Pruden, that this is of far more importance than nine thefts. To Bonaventure's as well as to the child."

"You don't care to explain?"

"I cannot possibly. I'm not being difficult, it is not clear to me yet, I can only compare it to reception being confused by static. But something is wrong."

Pruden was silent and then he said, "I'll telephone St. Bonaventure's and see what can be arranged."

When he called back ten minutes later it was to say that any interview would have to wait until Monday. "The office tells me that this morning the boy's father telephoned and asked that Gavin be sent home for the weekend. They're putting him on the four-o'clock train for Princeton."

"Isn't that rather unusual?"

"Yes, but the father was very firm."

Madame Karitska felt suddenly chilled. She said, "Bring him here before he leaves, will you?"

"Madame Karitska, for heaven's sake—"

"I think it can be managed if you yourself personally volunteer to escort him to the train afterward, don't you?"

"Look, I'm a busy man," growled Pruden.

"I believe you will find the stolen crosses hidden

somewhere in the chapel of St. Bonaventure's," she told him quietly. "You can tell me whether I'm correct when you bring the boy here at three o'clock." She hung up.

At three o'clock there was a knock on Madame Karitska's door and opening it she nodded to Pruden and then turned her attention to the young boy beside him. "Gavin?" she said lightly.

The boy nodded. He was slightly built, small for his fourteen years, with sensitive, finely drawn features in a face that was strikingly pale at the moment. "I have to get home," he told her edgily. "I'm wanted. Will this take long?"

"Come in, won't you? I want to talk to you, Gavin."

"Why?"

"I want you to go home tomorrow, or even later. I do not wish to see you go home tonight."

"Hey, now wait a minute," broke in Pruden.

Madame Karitska looked at him. "Gavin knows what I mean. Gavin knows exactly what I'm talking about, don't you, Gavin?"

The boy looked up at her in astonishment. Suddenly a look of infinite relief illuminated his face and he burst into tears. He walked into her arms and she held him.

"Let him cry," Madame Karitska said to Pruden, and over the boy's shoulder added, "Did you discover anything in the chapel?"

"Nothing yet, but they've only begun searching. Look, what is it with this boy? I talked to the school psychologist about him and he says he's unusually bright, stable, interested in his studies—"

"He's quite normal," said Madame Karitska, "but he

has one—deformity, shall we say? He's extremely psychic. I also get the impression looking at him that he's been severely punished for it as a child. It is not something he'd mention to anyone."

"In the meantime, if he stays here much longer it'll be kidnapping."

"Then arrest me," she said tartly.

"Look, all I did was ask you to examine fourteen rings—"

"The ways of God and karma are exceeding wondrous, are they not?"

"His parents—"

"Hush. If you know the parents' address you must send them a wire. Tell them he missed the train, tell them he has German measles, tell them he sprained his ankle. Tell them he will come tomorrow, or Sunday."

"Madame Karitska, for heaven's sake, I'm a policeman!"

She said stiffly, "I am a somewhat reputable person myself. Very well, give me their address and I shall send the wire myself. Gavin—?"

Sniffing and blowing his nose, Gavin blurted out the address. "But don't you think—oh, don't you think I *must* go?" he cried, beginning to tremble again.

Madame Karitska smiled tenderly at him. "We will speak of it later, Gavin. You are very tired but there is nothing you can do. It is cruel to say but true." To Pruden she said, "I will send the wire, don't worry. Come back this evening if you like, and see how we fare. In the meantime Gavin and I shall have some dinner, and I shall tell him stories about other people with the sixth sense. He may come to feel it not a sin or a crime after all."

"How did you know I thought it a sin?" asked Gavin.

"Ah—I too was once beaten for it," she assured him cheerfully.

By ten o'clock that evening Gavin was restless to the point of feverishness. "Oh please," he begged Madame Karitska. "It was my father who phoned, you know. Shouldn't I go home? *Shouldn't* I?"

"Perhaps you would care to talk about it now?"

The boy shivered. "No I can't, it's too horrible. I can't, and anyway it can't be true, I don't believe it."

She tucked him into bed and told him a few stories of yogis in the East. He was asleep when Pruden knocked at the door. It was late, nearly midnight.

"You must be very quiet," she cautioned him, letting him inside. "It's better for him to sleep."

Pruden threw himself across the couch and said almost angrily, "We found every one of the stolen items in the chapel. Every one of them except the chess pieces. It took hours and I'm exhausted."

"The chess pieces had crosses on them, didn't they?" asked Madame Karitska.

"Yes, but how the devil did you know that?"

At that moment a terrible cry came from the bedroom, the door was suddenly snatched open, almost torn from its hinges, and Gavin stood there with burning eyes. "I have to go home!" he shouted, and then he screamed, a terrible heart-rending scream, and fainted.

As Pruden caught the boy and laid him on the couch

Madame Karitska said in a quiet voice, "It is two minutes after midnight."

It was during his lunch hour the next day, twelve hours later, that Pruden brought her the newspaper and wearily handed it to her. "Second page, third paragraph," he said tonelessly, and sat down rather abruptly.

Madame Karitska read the words softly aloud. " 'MODEL FATHER KILLS FAMILY AND SELF. Five Dead in Princeton.' "

"Shortly after midnight," added Pruden in a strained voice. "Gavin's the only surviving member of the family, except nobody knew he'd survived until I told the Chief this morning that he's safe." He added savagely, "You knew?"

"No," she said calmly, "but Gavin did. It was his terror I picked up, his terror over something at his home."

" 'Model father,' it says," put in Pruden.

"Yes," said Madame Karitska sadly, "but what, after all, is a model, and who makes one? I suspect that at Christmas holidays Gavin sensed a change, a terrible change to despair. He sensed violence hanging over the house."

"But surely something could have been done—"

"How? Would you have believed him if he was capable of explaining?"

"But he wanted to go back—"

Madame Karitska sighed. "Because he is a very warm-hearted boy who loves his family, but if he had gone he would be dead too. I wonder if I have done him such a favor after all. So many gone!" She shook her head. "What will happen to Gavin now?"

"Well, I visited the school and they plan to offer Gavin anything he needs: legal guardianship, a scholarship, counseling, surrogate parents . . . a rather nice outfit, Bonaventure's. The Princeton police tell me there's an uncle too—his mother's brother—in the Peace Corps somewhere in Africa. He's flying back to handle things, but under the circumstances I believe Gavin's life will continue uninterrupted at Bonaventure's."

She nodded. "At least you can assure them, Lieutenant, that there will be no more thefts at the school. I can safely guarantee that now."

Pruden looked at her in astonishment. "You mean Gavin *did*—? You mean *he*—? But I thought you said—"

"When I first saw the list I began to wonder," she said. "I thought at first of someone with a fetish. Did you not find it odd that so many of the stolen objects were crosses? Perhaps you assumed they were stolen only because they had monetary value. Gavin took them for protection, not for profit."

"Protection?"

"The cross is still believed to be a protection against evil, is it not? Gavin believed he was doomed to die, and by some kind of demonic violence. Oh, he stole several other items to make it less obvious, but he stole the crosses to carry about with him on his person."

"But with all that he would have gone *willingly* home?" protested Pruden. "For God's sake, why?"

"How is your father these days?" asked Madame Karitska gently. "I trust he is recovering well?"

Pruden looked startled and then thoughtful, and was silent.

Chapter 6

Madame Karitska was going shopping this morning at Banmaker's, a delight very new to her, and although she intended to buy only a few yards of silk she had arranged her adventure as if it were a trip to Europe. She agreed with Gurdjieff, whom she had known at one point in her life, that one of the most important foods, second only to plant foods, was the ingestion of new impressions to stimulate and nourish the spirit. She chose to walk to the store by a route that was colorful to the eye, and upon arriving at Banmaker's she stood transfixed at the entrance, absorbing the marvels before her: broad aisles, brilliant lights and colors; books in bright jackets with letters fairly catapulting from the page to catch the eye; purses of leather and velvet and tapestry heaped in piles; a ribbon counter dazzling with stripes of fuchsia, melon, scarlet, pink, orange, blues.

Like a bazaar in Samarkand, she thought, taken back to her youth for a moment. Dreamily she began to stroll the aisles in search of her silks until bolt after bolt of rich fabric caught her eye near the Eighteenth Street entrance. As she moved toward them her mind was already sketching the long skirt she would cut and stitch out of an as-yet-unmet rainbow color. The essential problem behind frugality and poverty, she reflected, was that it denied such whims as these small ventures into elegance. She planned to feel very elegant indeed soon.

She fingered the materials: there was a taffeta that moved with a sound like running water, a velvet that lay warmly, solidly, in the hand. . . . Abruptly Madame Karitska turned, aware of a crackling hostility in the air, an almost physical feeling of tension nearby.

She saw a man standing not far away from her in the niche beside the elevators. He was solidly built, coatless, and narrow-eyed. He wore a dark suit with a carnation in his lapel and he stood his ground with an air of authority. His gaze was fixed upon someone in the aisle beyond. Turning further, Madame Karitska followed his gaze to the next aisle and saw that it was the jewelry counter. At one end a sleek woman in mink was slanting her head to study more closely the effect of a glittering bracelet on her wrist. The salesclerk fluttered over her effusively. At the other end of the counter a young man stood in front of a display of ornate necklaces.

There was no doubt that it was the young man who was under surveillance, and certainly his presence at such a counter was conspicuous. He wore bleached, mended blue-jeans and a wrinkled, navy-blue wool shirt. When he turned his head—rather furtively, thought Madame Karitska, as if to be sure no one was watching—she noted an unkempt dark beard. There was also a great deal of unkempt hair above the nape of his neck. He looked as if he had not washed in a week; he definitely looked as if he lacked the money to buy his lunch, yet he was rooted squarely in front of an array of semiprecious stones set artistically into silver. Oh, very suspicious indeed!

Impulsively Madame Karitska moved toward him, following silks into wools and then cottons. She arrived beside the young man just as he leaned over the glass surface that protected the necklaces, and just as he boldly pulled out half a dozen from beneath. His movement was so swift, so sure, that the necklaces were almost in his pocket before Madame Karitska could reach him.

Very sweetly she said, "Oh, thank you!" and firmly held his elbow to arrest the movement of necklaces to pocket. "Thank you so much," she said, forcing his arm into the air, where the necklaces dangled conspicuously. "I can see them so much better now."

She was aware of the young man's blind and frustrated fury, his catch of breath, and she was aware too of the floor detective's presence beside them. She continued to speak, saying thoughtfully, "Which do you think, Miroslav? The sapphires are lovely but a little too—shall we say, too baroque in that setting? The semiprecious stones are—" She paused and said to the store detective, "I beg your pardon, am I in your way?"

"He was stealing those," the man said accusingly.

The boy whirled, his anger turning to fear as he saw the man. A dark flush colored his cheeks. When he had finished looking at the store detective he turned back to Madame Karitska, his eyes baffled.

"I'll have to ask you both to come to my office," said the man.

Madame Karitska stood her ground. With equal coldness she said, "With or without the necklaces? If you think that Miroslav was planning to steal them, will you not count them, please? Here," she said contemptuously, drawing the necklaces from the young man's grasp. "Here, I insist that you count them. I shall not move. No, I will not, until you have made certain they are all *here*."

The detective gestured to the salesgirl. "The clerk will count them," he said stiffly, and handed them over to her. "My office, please."

"Look," said the young man awkwardly.

"Sssh," said Madame Karitska coldly, and preceded him to the office, where the detective asked for their names and addresses.

"John Painter," said the young man in a dispirited voice.

The store detective glanced up at Madame Karitska sharply. "You implied that you were shopping with him and yet you definitely called him by another name. And it wasn't John."

"No," said Madame Karitska calmly, "I called him Miroslav. I know his parents, and when they emigrated they Americanized their names, but actually he is Miroslav Khudoznik. Khudoznik is the Russian word for painter."

The young man stared at her in astonishment and

then had the good sense to wipe all expression from his face except for the faint trace of a grin that proved more difficult to erase.

"And your name?"

Madame Karitska gave it to him squarely. "The Countess Marina Elena Provovnitchek Gaylord Von Domm Karitska."

His eyes narrowed. "May I see some identification?"

Madame Karitska handed him her library card, her social security card, and her card of membership in the Balalaika Society.

"This address," he said, pointing to it. It was obvious that it subtracted a great deal from any impression a countess could make.

"Does my address or my integrity matter the more to you?" she asked coolly. "Ah, you want perhaps a voucher? Detective-Lieutenant Pruden of the Forty-first Precinct might be so kind as to speak for me."

For just a moment the detective's face looked human. He said dryly, picking up the telephone, "I only hope to God you didn't meet him professionally."

"But I did," Madame Karitska assured him blandly.

Half an hour later Madame Karitska and John Painter were allowed to leave the store, the young man having volunteered to have his pockets searched, and Lieutenant Pruden apparently having verified Madame Karitska's respectability. The store detective remained baffled but impotent.

"I think we do not speak, please, until we get outside," Madame Karitska told the young man firmly.

"What the hell, I *was* stealing those necklaces," he insisted upon blurting out.

"I know that," she said calmly. "It was as obvious to me as it was to him."

"Then why are you bailing me out?"

"Bailing?" asked Madame Karitska, frowning.

"Helping me."

"I liked your emanations," she explained to him.

He abruptly stopped, looking thoroughly alarmed. "My *what?*" he demanded in a shocked voice.

"Don't be narrow-minded," she told him scornfully. "I meant psychic emanations. Vibrations," she added impatiently. "Did you think I was purchasing your soul? Come and have a cup of coffee in this shop and tell me why you must steal six necklaces worth twenty-five dollars each when you have never stolen before in your life."

"How do you know I haven't?" he asked belligerently.

"I feel very impatient with you," she told him. "I have not bought the silks I came to buy, I have had to make up stories about you, and now you ask me how I know you have never stolen before. Have you?"

"No."

"Then why do you ask? That table over there looks pleasant."

They seated themselves in the coffee shop and Madame Karitska ordered coffee and buns for two. "Now—speak."

"I could just walk out and leave."

She looked at him. "Very true, and very childish. Why don't you?"

His eyes glinted appreciatively. "So I won't. Okay, I wanted to get my guitar out of hock."

"Hock," she repeated. "What is this word?"

"Pawnshop. My guitar's in the pawnshop."

Madame Karitska brightened; this she knew about. "Go on."

He shrugged. "I write songs. I had to pawn my guitar so I could stay home a few weeks and finish writing this new one. I wanted to finish it," he added defiantly.

"And did you?"

"Yeah, but now the rent's overdue, and I got a chance to play with a group tomorrow and pick up some bread—"

"Bread?"

"Cash. And I got no guitar and I'm flat."

"Please speak English."

He looked at her and grinned. "You think *you* speak it? Okay—sorry—I'm broke. No food money. No rent money. And now this chance to make a few bucks—dollars, I mean—and I'm trapped. So I thought —hell, all that jewelry. People with money to buy necklaces—well, I mean, what do they know or care about somebody like me?" He shrugged. "So okay, I turned criminal."

"Yes you did," she said calmly, "and one minute more and you would have lost your guitar, your freedom, and your job tomorrow night playing. My dear Mr.—"

"Khudoznik, wasn't it?" he said with his quick smile.

"Painter will do. I have known a few thieves in my day, and very clever ones, but you do not have either the nerve or the imagination for it. Look at you," she pointed out. "In a store like Banmaker's you must have been under scrutiny from the moment you entered."

He said dryly, "Buy me a suit and I'll go back and try again."

"Would you?" asked Madame Karitska coldly.

His face closed stubbornly.

Madame Karitska studied him a moment and then stood up. "Stay here," she said flatly. "I wish to call someone who might be interested in your situation."

She was gone for nearly ten minutes but when she returned the young man was still there. "You are to come to this address at seven o'clock this evening," she said, handing him a slip of paper. "If you come and met this gentleman—who is a man who may help you—you will perhaps have an opportunity to get your guitar back. I can promise nothing; it's up to you." She removed a bill from her wallet. "Get a shave and something to eat and wash your face."

He looked at her. "That goes with the deal?"

"Yes," she told him. "Do you think you can manage this?"

He thought about it and then grinned. "Well—not *comfortably*."

She nodded. "Then good-by until seven."

"Oh by the way," he said.

She turned.

He appeared to be struggling with something trapped in his throat; it turned out to be a word. "Thanks," he said.

Mr. Faber-Jones arrived five minutes before the hour, breathless and a little indignant. "This is insane," he said. "I don't know why I agreed to come. You've shortened my cocktail hour, delayed my dinner, and why do you live on such an appalling street? Who *is* this young man, anyway?"

Madame Karitska beamed at him. "I am indeed happy to see you again. You are still clairvoyant?"

He looked pained. "Please."

"Then you are still hoping it will go away?"

"Yes—and doing my best to drink away its departure. Now who *is* this chap?"

Madame Karitska lifted her voice. "Mr. Painter?" she called, and explained, "He arrived ten minutes ago. I sent him to the bathroom to wash his face. A clean shirt he managed—a tie, even—but not the clean face."

"Good Lord," said Faber-Jones weakly, and sat down.

The bathroom door swung open and Painter walked into the living room in his same ancient jeans but wearing a blazing pink shirt and purple tie. Madame Karitska looked with interest at Faber-Jones and was not disappointed: a look of absolute horror crossed his face. "Good God," he gasped.

"Mr. Faber-Jones—Mr. Painter," said Madame Karitska, amused and alert. To Faber-Jones she added, "I want you to look at him clairvoyantly, I want to see what you come up with."

"Must I?"

"I think so, yes."

"But he's wearing sneakers," groaned Faber-Jones.

"So he is, but I doubt that his psyche is wearing them," she said firmly. "Will you or won't you?"

"Will he what?" demanded Painter angrily.

"Look inside of you with a sixth sense."

"God," said Painter, looking from one to the other, "you're both kooks."

"I happen to be thinking the same of you," Faber-Jones told him indignantly. "All right, all right," he agreed testily. "Everybody be quiet and let me concentrate." He closed his eyes for a long moment and then opened them and narrowed them at Painter. He said in a startled voice, "Well, well!"

"Yes," said Madame Karitska. "His very soul has music. He is born to create it."

"*I* saw a gold phonograph record," admitted Faber-Jones.

"Oh?" said Madame Karitska. "But the situation is this: he has completed a song and his guitar is in hock —in the pawnshop, that is. He needs bread."

Faber-Jones drew out his wallet.

"I was thinking rather of your forming a record company," said Madame Karitska blandly.

"A what?" gasped Faber-Jones.

She shrugged. "Why not? This would be very good for both of you. Your own business is not going so well, and could be in serious trouble shortly, yet at the moment you have enough money to invest—"

Faber-Jones swallowed hard. "How do *you* know my business has been meeting with reverses?"

"How indeed?" said Madame Karitska, amused. "Come now, Mr. Faber-Jones, you have been a stock-broker who invests in new things, is this not right? And here is a talented young man who has written a fine song? Have you a copy?" she asked Painter.

He said uneasily, "It doesn't sound like anything much without my guitar."

"There, you see?" said Faber-Jones.

"Sing it then," said Madame Karitska.

He shook his head. "I can't sing without my guitar."

"Then let us read it," suggested Madame Karitska, and took the sheet of paper from him. "I'll read it aloud but of course it won't be the same."

She read:

> "Once in old Atlantis
> I loved a lady pure . . .
> And then the waters rose
> And death was black and cold.
>
> Once in Indian days
> I loved a maiden pure . . .
> But white men shot her through the heart
> And I was left to grieve.
>
> I saw her once in Auschwitz
> Young, dressed all in black . . .
> Our eyes met once beside the wall—
> The Nazis shot her dead.
>
> She's gone, I cannot find her
> A fortuneteller says 'Not yet . . .'
> For life's a slowly turning wheel
> And this turn's not for love."

There was silence and then Faber-Jones cried agonizingly, "It doesn't even rhyme!"

Madame Karitska was looking at young Painter with interest.

"And yet," Faber-Jones added in a puzzled voice, "it does have something. The thing is, what?"

"It's subliminal, no doubt," said Madame Karitska. "The subconscious is aware of many more things than we allow ourselves to know. You are intrigued enough to take the chance?"

Faber-Jones sighed. "I suppose so." He hesitated. "I don't doubt what I saw, it's just my getting connected with—I mean, he wears *sneakers.*"

"Be patient," said Madame Karitska sympathetically. "And *now* I believe you may get out your wallet, my friend, so that Mr. Painter can rescue his guitar. You were born under the sign of Pisces, were you not? Perhaps you can call your new company Pisces Recordings."

"Hey, not bad," said Painter.

Faber-Jones, counting out bills, only winced. "There," he said, giving them to John Painter. "Get your guitar and we'll see what should happen next." He glanced at Madame Karitska reproachfully and added, "You'll understand if I leave now, I hope? I'm expected at home for dinner and I'll be late even if I catch a taxi at your door." He hesitated and then, turning to Painter, said, "I can drop you off somewhere if you'd like. I'll give you my business address too, and we can work out an appointment tomorrow."

"Okay," said Painter, looking dazzled, and then with a grin at Madame Karitska he added, "sir," and gave her a humorous little salute as he turned to follow Faber-Jones.

Chapter 7

Madame Karitska had invited Lieutenant Pruden to dine with her—a simple Hungarian goulash with spaetzls, she said—and he arrived at seven, bringing with him a bottle of red wine.

"But such a fine wine," she exclaimed, holding it to the light. "It has been a long time since I have seen this."

"Well," Pruden said, flushing slightly, "I asked the man at the shop what he'd recommend for a distinguished lady of Russian extraction who was serving goulash. He said he would first of all recommend my bringing *him* along to dinner too, and, if not that, a worthy bottle like this one. Myself, I'm a beer man."

She laughed, but her glance, moving from the wine bottle to his face, sharpened. "Something is troubling you, I think, and it is not the wine."

He grinned. "I wish you'd stop reading my mind. Anyway, nothing should interfere with goulash; it's a favorite of mine."

"Good. We speak of it later then," she told him.

She had placed a card table with a checkered cloth over it near the windows, and had drawn the curtains and lighted candles. There were even two wilted white roses in a bud vase. "Plucked from a basket of trash on Walnut Street," she said with a smile. "It remains incredible to me what things of value are tossed away on Walnut Street." Sitting down to dine they began to talk about Walnut Street, and then about other parts of the city, which Pruden knew thoroughly and obviously loved.

Over the demitasse Madame Karitska inserted a cigarette into a long gray holder and looked at him frankly. "You have told me many things about this city and your work, Lieutenant, but always there lurks the faint shadow behind your eyes. It has to do with your job?"

"Unfortunately not any longer," he said.

She was at once sympathetic. "You have perhaps been taken off a case?"

He sighed. "In a way, yes, but not by anyone in the department. I learned late this afternoon—it'll be in the newspapers tomorrow, undoubtedly on a back page—that a woman named Mazda Lorvale died in a mental hospital today, apparently a suicide."

"This is very sad," said Madame Karitska. "You knew her?"

"I handled the case three years ago. It was never solved and now I don't suppose it ever will be, and I'll wonder for the rest of my life if she was guilty or innocent." He lifted his gaze from the coffee and added, "One does, you know."

"Why don't you tell me about it?" suggested Madame Karitska.

He said impulsively, "I'll do more than that if you'll allow me. It's a hell of a way to thank you for a delicious goulash-and-spaetzl dinner, but knowing I was coming here I smuggled her suicide note out of headquarters. I'd give a great deal to know whether she really killed three people. If you can tell such a thing by examining the note."

"Three people," mused Madame Karitska. "I think perhaps you must first tell me her story."

"All right. You know the Dell section of Trafton? It's on the outskirts of the city, a very modest suburb: frame houses, tiny immaculate lawns, vegetable gardens and clotheslines in the rear. Basically it's a Ukrainian neighborhood, with a Russian Orthodox church in its center, like the hub of a wheel."

"I know," said Madame Karitska, nodding. "I have seen the church."

"Well, three years ago a man from the Dell section was rushed to the hospital here in Trafton. His name was Charles Windham, he was sixty-seven, retired, a widower, and he lived alone at 52½ Arbor Street. He was dead on arrival, and the lab established that he'd died of cyanide poisoning.

"Two days later a forty-one-year-old woman was found dead in her home at 48½ Arbor Street, two houses removed from Windham's home. Her name, if I remember correctly, was Polly Biggs and it was discovered that she too had died of cyanide poisoning."

"Ah," said Madame Karitska, nodding.

"Swope was assigned to the investigation at that time. Myself, I was busy investigating the disappearance of a professor from Trafton University named Dr. Ulanov Bugov. This man lived across town near the university campus and he'd not returned to his Russian history classes. Much to my surprise, in investigating his disappearance, I discovered that he'd been a fairly regular visitor on Arbor Street. He'd sent Christmas cards to both of the deceased, and he'd been very friendly with the woman who lived alone at number 50, whose house was between Polly Biggs's and Windham's. This was Mazda Lorvale.

"Swope had been checking out Mazda Lorvale, as he had all the neighbors. Now we discovered that someone in that neighborhood had pawned Dr. Bugov's gold watch. The pawnbroker gave us a very precise description of the woman who had pawned it, and it exactly matched that of Mazda Lorvale. Next the bank produced several checks made out to Mazda and signed by Dr. Bugov several days *after his disappearance*. These checks proved to be forgeries, and Mazda had forged them."

"So she was arrested," said Madame Karitska.

"Not then. We first had a warrant issued and searched her house. We hit pay dirt all right. We found Dr. Bugov's attaché case under her bed, his checkbook in her bureau drawer, and a quantity of cyanide hidden away in her pantry. That's when she was arrested on suspicion of murdering Charles Windham and Polly Biggs, but of course we felt pretty sure by that time that she must have murdered Dr. Bugov too."

"But you say she has just died in a mental hospital?"

Pruden nodded. "She was put on trial for the two poison murders while we continued searching for Dr. Bugov's body. We even dug up the basement of her house. We had men searching the grounds of every nearby park, looking under culverts, and checking every piece of empty ground in the Dell section. The professor," he said with finality, "was never found, dead or alive."

"Extraordinary," said Madame Karitska with interest. "And in this trial, was she found guilty?"

He shook his head. "It was a long trial, a rather sensational one at the time, but if it had been concluded, I seriously doubt that a verdict of guilty would have been brought in. There just wasn't enough evidence, certainly nothing conclusive. She'd forged his name to those checks, yes, and she'd pawned his gold watch but there was no binding evidence of murder. She'd known Dr. Bugov for two years, we established that, but we never discovered how they met. There was the possibility that they'd been lovers—he was forty, she was thirty-five and quite attractive in a candy-box way. But when it came time for her to testify—they put her on the stand—she was rambling and incoherent, and made wild, extreme statements. She had to be removed from the stand. Ultimately the jury found her legally insane and she was ordered confined."

"So the truth was never unearthed," said Madame Karitska thoughtfully. "A strange story. She denied the murders?"

"Oh yes, and denies them even in her suicide note." He removed a brown manila envelope from his pocket and carefully extracted a note written in pencil on lined notebook paper. "The note was written to the lawyer

who defended her three years ago and it reads, 'It doesn't matter really but I will say this. I didn't kill Uli or Polly or Charlie. I went wild with grief from losing them. Nothing has been worth anything since.' "
He handed the slip of paper to Madame Karitska and sat back.

Madame Karitska placed the letter on the table and gently inserted her fingers under it until the letter rested across the palms of her hands. After a moment she closed her eyes and Pruden sat in silence, watching her. The candles flickered and wavered; in the dim light he thought Madame Karitska's face looked infinitely sad. When she opened her eyes her expression was thoughtful.

"Well?" asked Pruden.

"Tell me," she said, putting down the note, "would there be any possible way to bring me—at this late date—any objects handled by Dr. Bugov or by this Polly Biggs or Charles Windham?"

Pruden was startled. "That's a rather tall order after three years. It's possible, though, I suppose. Dr. Bugov's papers are still somewhere at headquarters— we sifted through them all for leads but found nothing. And Mrs. Biggs's mother carried away Polly's jewelry and is in a nursing home not far off my route. As for Mr. Windham—"

"That would be quite enough," Madame Karitska told him.

Pruden smiled. "You're not going to tell me any impressions you received, as you put it?"

"No," said Madame Karitska. "Not tonight."

"But you did catch something?" he asked eagerly.

"Oh yes," she said, "a great deal, and I am most

curious. If you will bring me objects belonging to two of the three persons I think I may be able to tie certain threads together for you. Your case," she added with a faint smile, "is not yet over."

It was two days before Pruden reappeared, looking triumphant, which was not surprising because it had taken a certain amount of resourcefulness and digging to produce the objects he presented to her. He gave her the gold watch belonging to Dr. Bugov that had been pawned by Mazda Lorvale, and which was still marked "Exhibit B" from the trial, and a leather checkbook of his as well. From Polly Biggs's mother he had secured a ring and a silver necklace. He placed them on the carved wooden table in the center of the room and then noticed a neatly clipped newspaper item already there. He picked it up.

"MYSTERY FIGURE APPARENT SUICIDE," he read aloud. "I thought you didn't read newspapers, Madame Karitska."

"I don't usually," she admitted, "but you said the story would be carried in the newspapers today and I was most curious to read a second version of her trial and the murders. For instance," she said, "you did not tell me how Mazda 'babbled,' as the paper expresses it, of knowing influential people in very high places, and of doing important intelligence work."

Pruden shrugged. "That's one of the reasons she was judged insane. I told you she grew incoherent at the trial. An uneducated, simple woman ranting and raving—"

"Exactly," said Madame Karitska, and sat down and picked up Dr. Bugov's watch and held it in her hand. She sat bemused for some length of time, nodded several times, removed the watch and picked up the ring and necklace. After several minutes she removed them and restored the watch to her hand.

At last, looking somber, she put down the watch and walked into the kitchen to return with a pot of Turkish coffee. Abruptly she said, "I will tell you now. Your Mazda Lorvale was innocent."

"Oh God," said Pruden.

"She was not insane either," said Madame Karitska, pouring coffee into two cups.

Pruden stared at her blankly. "Now you've surely gone too far; you've got to be kidding."

"I do not, as you say, 'kid,' " she told him distastefully. "You described this woman to me yourself only a few moments ago. You called her an uneducated, simple woman, and this is precisely what her suicide note has told me. She lived in much agony, poor woman, and probably never fully understood what happened to her. Her intelligence, you see, was below average. She was not stupid, you understand, or retarded in the physical sense, but her intelligence was limited—stunted, probably, by overwhelming emotional deprivation in her childhood. She was, in a word, the perfect dupe."

"Dupe?" echoed Pruden incredulously.

"It astonishes me that no one paid any attention to her so-called babblings about doing important work. She believed it, didn't anyone realize this? She was not insane and she believed it, but why did she believe it?"

Pruden looked astonished and then interested. "I don't understand."

Madame Karitska picked up Dr. Bugov's gold watch and held it lightly in her hand. "The man to whom this belonged was not born in this country. From his watch I gain the impression of a man of ice, a man callous and devious and brilliant of intellect. I do not think you will ever find the body of Dr. Bugov, Lieutenant. I believe he is still very much alive."

"Alive!"

"Yes, under a new name, no doubt, but alive. *He* is the man who poisoned your Mrs. Biggs and Mr. Windham."

"Biggs and Windham! But why?" protested Pruden.

"To rid himself of Mazda Lorvale," she said. "She babbled about doing important intelligence work at her trial but no one wondered why. *He* is the man who was doing the important intelligence work, Lieutenant, although I doubt seriously that it was for this country. You have here a love-starved woman of modest good looks, submissive disposition, and low intelligence. It is just the sort of woman this man can use, even confide in for he could never risk intimacy with a peer. Mazda becomes his mistress, his slave, you might say. With her he can let down a little, relax, brag a little, and to her he is the sun, the moon, and the stars. She gives herself heart, body, and soul, you understand? It is very sad."

Pruden stared at her, dazed. "But the others— Biggs and Windham?"

She nodded. "He is very clever, do you not think so, your Dr. Bugov? The time comes for him to break up this constricting alliance. He has grown bored, perhaps, or the liaison has become dangerous, but it is more likely that he has received orders to go elsewhere. How then is he to dispose of this poor creature who would be an embarrassment and a danger to him when he has left?"

She shrugged before continuing. "To kill her directly I think would be too risky. He has been perhaps a little too open; he has become known to her friends and the trail would lead straight to him. So instead he poisons first one and then another of Mazda's neighbors and thus he disposes of two witnesses to their relationship and throws suspicion squarely on Mazda."

"And the watch, the checks?"

"He leaves them with her, of course, or, as you police say, plants them upon her? Perhaps he has even encouraged her to sign his checks for him. He then disappears, thus in every way tightening the noose about her neck."

"Good God," he said faintly.

She nodded. "Yes, I feel for this bewildered woman. Her suicide note struck you as sincere? It is a very sad note. And this man—"

"This man," said Lieutenant Pruden grimly.

"I would hope," she said gently, "that among the many things you have of his, there may be a fingerprint or two remaining that belong to him. This checkbook, for instance, or something untouched among the possessions you hold. It would be wise to present these prints to a much higher government agency to see if there are any records, any prints that match. A simple professor at a university who disappears does not merit such research but the man behind this façade—"

"I get your point," Pruden said grimly, and then, with a shake of his head, "You make it sound so simple."

"Simple?" She looked at him in surprise. "It is like

a kaleidoscope, that is all. A small shift of focus and one sees beyond illusion to reality. You look at things one way, I another, but you need only shift your attention and you too will see."

"Well, if it should be true—" He put down his napkin. "I think you will forgive me if I leave now, Madame Karitska, I think there is a little unfinished business I should look into tonight."

"I think so too," she said with a twinkle. "And we will see, shall we not?"

They did not meet again until the weekend, but when Pruden arrived he still had not lost the slightly dazed look that he had worn five nights earlier. He stood in the doorway and said, "I've just visited Mazda's grave. I think I went to—no, I don't know why I went."

"No?" she said smiling.

"Interpol finally identified his fingerprints," he said harshly. "He was never Ulanov Bugov. They don't know who he is, except they have his fingerprints and about half a dozen aliases. I thought you'd want to know."

"Yes."

He nodded and turned away. "There were flowers on her grave today," he said, suddenly turning back. "Nobody attended her funeral, they tell me, and yet there were flowers on her grave today."

"As I believe I said before," Madame Karitska told him gravely, "it continues to astonish me what things of value are thrown away on Walnut Street."

Chapter 8

"What's this?" asked Pruden, stopping in at Madame Karitska's one evening on his way home after a long day on the street. He had just discovered that Madame Karitska had two guests, one of them Gavin O'Connell, the other a very Establishment-type middle-aged man in a well-cut business suit.

Madame Karitska put a finger to her lips and gestured him to follow her to the center of the room. Lieutenant Pruden could make no sense of what he saw. Neither Gavin nor the stranger appeared even aware of his arrival: in front of each lay a book, and they were staring with enormous concentration at their respective half-open volumes.

And suddenly as he watched a strange thing happened: a page of Gavin's book slowly lifted and turned. There were no windows open: there were no hands touching the pages and yet the page had turned.

"I did it," crowed Gavin gleefully. "Hey, Jonesy, I did it!"

"Mr. Faber-Jones, this is Lieutenant Pruden," broke in Madame Karitska. "Yes, you did it, Gavin. Capital! But Mr. Faber-Jones also had some success, I notice."

"Kind of you," said Faber-Jones, getting to his feet. "Only pushed the page halfway, though, and frankly I'm exhausted."

"Me too," admitted Gavin. "Hi, Lieutenant Pruden!"

"What have I interrupted?" asked Pruden curiously.

"A practice session," Gavin told him eagerly. "It's great meeting Mr. Faber-Jones, you know, he has the gift too."

"Oh? But what have you been practicing?"

"Concentration," said Madame Karitska. "The moving of mountains by the use of the mind. In this case, the lifting of a page in a book by sheer concentration of psychic energies. The pages can turn—you saw it yourself."

"Incredible," said Pruden.

"You can't just say 'Move!' to the pages either," put in Gavin. "You have to lift them with concentrated *thought*, and boy it's rough. It's fun too, though. You ought to try it."

Pruden's laugh was short and doubting.

"You find it unbelievable?" inquired Madame Karitska.

"I don't know," said Pruden, frowning. "I might have six days ago but—"

"But what?" asked Faber-Jones, sinking into the couch, obviously tired and ready for diversion.

"Do not say a word," said Madame Karitska, "until

I bring out the Turkish coffee I've brewed, with a glass of milk for Gavin." When she had returned and distributed refreshments she sat down and inserted a cigarette into a long holder. "Now tell us what has placed a crack in your imperviousness."

Pruden said, "I'd really like to know: you believe the mind has such intensity, such power?"

"But of course," she said, amused. "We use only a fraction of its power, we use only a tiny amount of ourselves."

"But for instance," Pruden said, picking his words carefully, "do you believe a man can simply announce that he's going to die, be in perfect health and—just die?"

Madame Karitska smiled faintly. "So many diseases are psychosomatic, it happens oftener than you think. I have seen people turn their faces from life, their will to live gone. It may take months or years but they die."

He shook his head. "I mean something much faster than that—death in a matter of days."

"Ah," said Madame Karitska, "now that is very interesting. You have met such a situation? You must have met such a situation or you would not be speaking of this?"

He said ruefully, "I'm still not accustomed to having my mind browsed through but yes, I've met such a situation. Heard about it, at least. The patrolman on the block, Bill Kane, has been puzzling over it for days. It seems a man named Arturo Mendez died about two weeks ago. On a Wednesday he told his brother Luis that he would die before the week was out, and on the following Tuesday night he died."

"Did they not call a doctor?"

"On Monday they called an ambulance and he was taken to the hospital. The doctors found nothing organically wrong with him, but the following night he was dead."

"Did they perform an autopsy?"

Pruden nodded. "He died quite literally of a heart stoppage but there was nothing wrong with his heart either."

"Then it was precognition," put in Gavin eagerly. "He knew something was going to happen ahead of time."

"No—no, I think not," Madame Karitska said, and with an intent glance at Pruden, "There is more?"

He nodded. "Yesterday Bill Kane told me that Arturo's brother Luis won't get out of bed now. He's settled his debts, paid his landlady a week's rent in advance, and told her that he'll be dead by Monday morning."

"And this is Friday night," mused Madame Karitska. "I wonder . . . where do they live, Lieutenant?"

"Three blocks away on Fifth Street, in the Puerto Rican section."

She nodded. "I will go there tomorrow, I would like to see this."

Pruden shook his head. "It's not a good section for gringos, as they call us. Very few speak English, and Luis only a little. Do you speak Spanish?"

"No," said Madame Karitska, "but there is communication without speech." She added thoughtfully, "This is very interesting to me. There are yogis in the East, of course, who can stop breathing at will, but neither of your two men is a yogi; there must be very powerful forces involved here. It is the invisible at work, and I am a student of the invisible." She glanced abruptly at her watch and said, "It's time, Gavin." To Pruden she explained, "Mr. Faber-Jones has brought over a portable television so that we can see John Painter make his debut on the 'Tommy Tompkins Show.' "

"Someone you know?" asked Pruden as Gavin jumped up to turn on the set.

"A protégé of Mr. Faber-Jones."

Faber-Jones looked at her reproachfully. "We both know whose protégé he really is, Madame Karitska."

"Nonsense," she told him, "you're growing quite fond of him and you know it, especially since he stopped wearing tennis sneakers."

"He only exchanged them for calfskin boots and a sequin jump suit," put in Faber-Jones dryly. "A very expensive sequin jump suit too, I might add."

"Hey, that sounds cool," broke in Gavin. "You think I could meet him sometime?"

"Sssh," said Madame Karitska, touching his shoulder and pointing to the television screen on which a glowing sequinned figure had appeared, guitar in hand, to sit on a stool in front of the cameras. Faber-Jones turned up the volume just as the song began:

> "Once in old Atlantis
>   I loved a lady pure . . .
>   And then the waters rose . . ."

"It's already number two on the charts," Faber-Jones told Pruden in an aside. "My Pisces company cut the platter."

"Oh?" said Pruden, blinking, and gave Faber-Jones a startled second glance.

On the following morning Madame Karitska had an appointment at nine o'clock, and when her client had left she placed a sign on her door that read BACK AT 12. She then set out for Fifth Street, which she had always enjoyed on her walks around the city because so much of its life was lived without concealment on the street. Today was no exception: the sun was summer-hot and before Madame Karitska had even reached Fifth Street she could hear its music. At this hour flamenco dominated, and then as she rounded the corner she was met by John Painter's "Once in Old Atlantis" pouring out of the Caballeros Social Club across the street.

Madame Karitska picked her way along the crowded sidewalk. Street vendors chanted and shouted, and young men armed with lugs and wrenches peered into the hoods of old cars or lay under them with only sandaled feet showing. Several old men huddled over a game spread out on empty orange crates, and one family of four were unself-consciously eating early lunch at a card table on the sidewalk. Every stair and porch was occupied by people of varying ages taking the sun with the enthusiasm of any Miami Beach sunlounger. It was noisy, but it was more alive than Walnut Street could ever be.

As Madame Karitska approached number 203 a uniformed policeman came out of a store across the street, saw her, and waved. Crossing to her side he said, "You must be the lady Lieutenant Pruden said would be coming around ten to see Luis. I've been watching for you, I'm Bill Kane."

They shook hands. "I told his landlady I'd be bringing you over," he added. Her name's Mrs. Malone."

"Malone!" said Madame Karitska, amused. "Lieutenant Pruden was certain no one would speak English here."

"The lieutenant's not a patrolman, he only drives through in a car," Kane said forgivingly. "Mrs. Malone's been here for years, runs a very tight boarding-house. This area," he said, pointing, "runs ten blocks down to the river. Used to be Irish, now it's Puerto Rican."

He stopped in front of a narrow clapboard house painted a dull brown. Narrow wooden steps led up to a narrow front porch made narrower by two windows with starched lace curtains and a heavy wooden door with a peephole. Patrolman Kane rang, and after an interval they heard approaching footsteps inside. The door swung open and a large woman with round pink cheeks and black hair confronted them. Her face softened when she saw Bill Kane. "Well, now, so it's you," she said, beaming at them both. "I didn't even have time to take off my apron, I was that busy baking, you see. Come in, come in."

"And we won't keep you from your baking more than a moment," Madame Karitska told her reassuringly. "We've come to see Luis Mendez."

"Well, it's kind of you, I'm sure. A terrible business, this, I can tell you. He won't eat," said Mrs. Malone, crossing herself. "His girl friend Maria sits with him evenings but everybody else stays away. They're scared. It scares me too, frankly."

"Yes," said Madame Karitska as they began climb-

ing steep carpeted stairs. "Does he have many friends?
Is he well-liked?"

"Oh, he's very popular in the neighborhood," said
Mrs. Malone. "He drives an ice-cream truck, you know,
or did—and his brother too, God rest his soul—and
very hard-working and personable they was too. A very
nice way they had about them with children. 'Hey!
Here comes Looie. *Viva* Looie,'" she said with a shift
into mimicry. "Many's the time I'd hear them. The
kids loved him. As for close friends," she added in a
practical voice, "well, they've been here in the States
only two years and more hard-working men I've never
seen. Up at dawn, back late—but," she said with a
twinkle, "I'm not saying there wasn't time for a few
beers at the social club, or time for a girl friend. Very
good men, both of 'em. Hard-working and kind."

"No enemies?" emphasized Madame Karitska.

"Enemies!" Mrs. Malone's shocked voice was reply
enough. "Luis? Goodness no!" She opened the door
of a room at the end of the hall and called, "Company
for you, Mr. Mendez. Not that he'll hear me," she
added in an aside. "Real spooky it is."

They entered a large room, sparely furnished. The
walls were papered with garish climbing roses that
nearly obscured two crucifixes hung on the wall. There
was a huge overstuffed chair in one corner, with a lamp
and magazine table beside it. The bureau was massive
and bore a statue of the Virgin Mary as well as a great
deal of clutter. On a double bed by the window lay a
young man in a rumpled shirt and slacks, his eyes
open and staring at the ceiling. He looked no more
than thirty, with jet-black hair and a black stubble of
beard along his jaw, but the color had been drained

from his skin, leaving it gray, and there were dull blue smudges under his eyes.

The landlady withdrew, closing the door behind her, and Bill Kane stood with his back to it, like a guard. Madame Karitska walked over to the bed, looked down into the man's face and then sat on the edge of the bed and grasped one of his hands in hers. She said nothing. The man's gaze swerved to hers and he moved restlessly, rebelliously.

"Can you speak?" she asked softly.

He groaned. *"Si*—go away." He snatched his hand away from hers and turned his face to the wall.

"He sure has the look of death on him," said Kane in a low voice. "It's uncanny."

"Yes? Well, we shall see," she said, and walked over to the bureau to glance at the many objects abandoned there. One in particular drew her attention; a black candle shaped like a man, six inches high and standing upright in a saucer. Several broken matches lay beside it. She picked up the saucer and thoughtfully examined the candle, then put it down and glanced at an elaborately framed photograph of a beautiful girl. An inscription in the corner read, "All my love, Maria."

She nodded. "We can go now," she said.

"Already?" Kane was startled. "I thought—well, frankly the lieutenant made it sound as if you could cure Luis."

Madame Karitska was amused. "I only diagnose, I cannot cure."

"Well, then," said Kane, brightening, "what did you decide about Luis?"

"That this is a case for Lieutenant Pruden and that we should call him at once," she told him crisply. "This man is being murdered, and the lieutenant handles homicides, does he not?"

"What do you mean, he's being murdered?" demanded Pruden, climbing out of a patrol car in front of Mrs. Malone's boardinghouse. "A man decides he wants to die it's suicide, not murder."

"When you have finished losing your temper," said Madame Karitska calmly, "I will explain to you why Luis Mendez is not committing suicide. In the meantime let us walk to the Botanica around the corner and see what we can do to save his life."

"You might call a doctor first," he said irritably, falling into step beside her.

"A doctor cannot possibly help him," she told him. "This is *espiritismo*. Here we are," she added, turning the corner, and came to a stop in front of LeCruz' West Indies Botanica.

"This place?" protested Pruden. On display in the window were statues of Buddha, of the Virgin Mary, and of figures he'd never seen before, some of them grotesque, some of them appealing; holy medals lying in nests of velvet, herb-burners fashioned of pottery, and plastic bottles advertised as ritual lotions. Madame Karitska opened the door, a bell jangled, and a gnarled little man with white hair and heavily pouched eyes glanced up from the counter. "Ah, Madame Karitska," he said, brightening. "How nice to see you again."

"The pleasure is mine," Madame Karitska told him warmly, shaking his hand. "You are well? Your family is well?"

"We are all well, Madame Karitska. And you?"

"In need of help, Mr. LeCruz. I know you have

several spiritists among your clientele and we urgently need the best. Can you recommend one?"

Mr. LeCruz' glance moved to Pruden and rested on him doubtfully. "For me to recommend—I am not sure this is wise."

"I can vouch for Mr. Pruden," she said with a smile. "He is no believer but I am educating him, Mr. Le-Cruz."

He nodded. "Okay then." He was thoughtful a moment, then brought out paper and pencil. "I give you two names with addresses."

With a nod toward the shelves Pruden said, "What's all this—uh—merchandise?"

"I'll show you," Madame Karitska said, and taking his arm guided him along the counter. "Here you see candles: red ones to attract a loved one, blue candles for healing, yellow and white when communication with the dead is wished. And here is a black Chango candle," she added, picking one up. She handed it to Pruden and he stared blankly at the shape of a male figure about six inches tall. "It's burned when one hopes for the death of an enemy," she told him, and added casually, "I have been told Luis Mendez has no enemies, but there is a black Chango candle like this on the bureau in his room."

"Oh for heaven's sake," protested Pruden.

She went on, ignoring the slant of his brows. "Here you see black rag dolls with gold-plated needles—oh dear, eight dollars now, the price is going up. As you probably know, the needles are struck into the dolls to cause pain to enemies. And here are herbs, a very fine selection, each for different purposes, and although Mr. LeCruz disapproves of black magic he is a man who also likes to pay his bills and so you find here vials of snake oil, graveyard dust, and bats' blood."

Pruden groaned. "Please. I was back at headquarters making out reports, and you pulled me away for this? I thought—"

"Ah, Mr. LeCruz is waiting for us," she said, interrupting him, and moved toward him with a smile.

"I've given you two names," Mr. LeCruz told her in a low voice. "Each from different cults. Both are fine, I hear, and give good results."

"Results are what we need. Thank you, Mr. LeCruz," she said, and to Pruden, "Shall we go now? I'll explain outside what I discovered and then you can go back to your reports at headquarters."

"While you go to Third Street?" he said, glancing at the addresses on the sheet of paper. "Not on your life, I'm going with you. People like you get mugged on Third Street."

"If you go with me you will have to forget that you are a policeman," she told him sternly. "You're not dressed as one, so if you'll not speak like one or act like one—"

"Why?"

"Because there will be nothing rational about this, my dear Lieutenant, but then there is so much in life that isn't. The important thing—of the highest order— is to save Mendez' life. Then you must proceed as with any attempted murder, and discover who wishes the Mendez brothers dead."

"And the weapon?" he asked, amused.

"The mind."

"I don't think you can convict anyone on that," he told her dryly.

"Exactly," she said in her clear crisp voice. "Which makes it very clever, do you not think so? The perfect crime."

He'd not thought of it in this light. "You really think that?" he said, his brows slanting. "Of course if it could be done, if it were possible—"

"My dear Lieutenant," she told him with a smile, "voodoo is a religion older than Christianity. You have seen far too many Hollywood movies, I think. It is as old as astronomy, and uses astronomy in its beliefs and its gods, and it has many similarities to Christianity. It is a complex, ancient, and very structured religion, with formal rites and ceremonies, a culture as well as a religion. Don't, as John Painter would say, knock it."

"Obviously I mustn't," he said meekly.

They entered Third Street, a desolate street with windows broken in many of its buildings. A few black children playing hopscotch on the sidewalk stopped and stared at them; an old man sitting on a step in the sun bowed a grayed head to them as they passed. Farther along the street rock-and-roll music poured from a delicatessen around which at least a dozen young men idled.

"Here is number 180," said Madame Karitska, and they confronted high narrow steps to an open door, beyond which rose a second flight to the floor above. "She is called Madame Souffrant."

"Madame, eh?" said Pruden with a grin.

A cardboard sign just inside the door bore the name, with a purple arrow pointing to the second floor. They climbed rickety stairs and knocked at a door. A stately West Indian woman, her skin the color of café crème, answered their knock.

Madame Karitska said briskly, "A man is dying on Fifth Street; he's possessed and needs a spiritist. He has said he will die Monday morning."

"And this is Saturday noon," the woman said, nodding. "What cult?"

"I don't know but he came here from Puerto Rico two years ago. Mr. LeCruz gave us your name and that of a Miss Loaquin. Do you think you can help him?"

"Come in," said Madame Souffrant.

They entered a room with floors that slanted alarmingly but the room itself was clean to the point of sterility; the linoleum rug shone with polish, the long couch along the wall was covered with transparent plastic and plastic roses bloomed everywhere. "Sit down," said Madame Souffrant. "I think you need look no further, but I'll go back with you first and see the man to be certain."

"You can arrange the ritual for today, perhaps?" asked Madame Karitska.

"It can be done." The woman peered into the kitchen, spoke to someone, and closed the door. "My cat," she explained, and picking up a small suitcase resembling a doctor's bag she gestured to them to precede her, and locked the door behind her.

Pruden, with the feeling that none of this could be real, escorted them back to Fifth Street.

"You will come in?" asked Madame Karitska at the steps of Mrs. Malone's boardinghouse.

Pruden shook his head. "You said it's impossible to question Luis Mendez so I'll make a few inquiries of his girl friend instead. But only," he added pointedly, "if you continue to insist this is murder."

She regarded him with sympathy but with some impatience as well. "I insist, yes."

Pruden found Luis' girl friend at the Grecian Beauty Shoppe on Seventh Street. Maria Ardizzone was her name, with a very lovely Italian face to go with it, curly hair down to her shoulders and liquid black eyes. She was plump and would run to fat in a few years, but there was poise and ambition here, he thought, as he watched her take command of the interview with the ease of a girl who knew what she wanted. What she wanted, apparently, was Luis Mendez and a number of small Mendezes, and what she most admired about Luis was his ambition and his drive.

"But his sickness I do not understand," she said, faltering for the first time. "I do not understand this at all. The men in my family, they get the flu, they break an arm, they keep working. Luis, he just lies down. It is not *like* Luis; he works hard, he has built a good business."

"Doing what?" asked Pruden.

"They own—owned—two Jack Frost ice-cream trucks."

"Ice-cream trucks," repeated Pruden, frowning.

Maria nodded, her long rippling black hair nodding with her. "They scrimp, they save, they buy one truck. That was when I first met Luis. The truck they buy from Mr. Materas, the distributor, and Luis he drove it while Arturo took any job he could get to save up and buy the second one. Luis, he made three hundred dollars a day and do you think he would spend a nickel on himself? No, every penny went to buy the second truck free and clear. One must admire a man like that, Lieutenant," she said frankly.

"Yes indeed," murmured Pruden.

"I help them with the books," she added proudly. "April to October they sold the ice cream, and last year Arturo, he made fifteen thousand dollars for the year and Luis—my Luis, he made eighteen thousand dollars."

"That's a good living on Fifth Street," put in Pruden.

She nodded. "Yes, this is very good. Luis was happy, he felt good, and then Arturo died and—" She shook her head, her luminous eyes turning into wells of sadness. "Since then everything has been bad," she said simply. "Now Luis says he too must die."

" 'Must?' " quoted Pruden.

"That is how he said it. It is strange, isn't it?"

"Surely something must have happened to make him say that. Did anything discourage him?"

"Nothing, I tell you."

"No enemies?"

Her eyes blazed. "Luis? Luis had only *friends*."

Pruden tried a new tack. "Was there anything unusual, then, no matter how small or unimportant, that happened about that time?"

She hesitated, and he thought her eyes flickered before she shook her head. "There was nothing."

He nodded. "Then I won't keep you from your customers any longer, Miss Ardizzone, but I may come back to ask you a few more questions."

"Please—any time," she told him. "Anything that will help Luis. I would give my life for Luis," she said fiercely. "You believe he can be helped?"

"I know someone who thinks so."

"Then I will light candles for them," she said. "For

them as well as Luis. I will kiss their hands and their feet."

"Yes," said Pruden, blinking at her passion. He tried to picture Madame Karitska's reaction to having her hands and feet kissed, and he left before a smile could reach his lips. He didn't return to Fifth Street, however; he went back to headquarters to see Donnelly, who had a memory like a computer bank.

"Don, I want you to tell me about ice-cream trucks."

"They sell ice cream," Donnelly pointed out sourly.

Pruden ignored this. "I'm up against a dead man and one dying man who have no enemies but happen to own and drive ice-cream trucks. It's the only lead I've got at the moment. Look, a few years ago there was some trouble, wasn't there? Muscle stuff?"

Donnelly nodded. "You bet your sweet life there was. It was over in the Dell section two years ago. Parts stolen, one driver kidnapped, ten trucks blown up. A real war over the territory."

"Who won?"

"*They* did, we think. Suddenly all the trouble stopped and nobody would talk."

"And who's 'they?' "

Donnelly regarded him laconically. " 'They' are not us, Lieutenant."

Pruden nodded. "How do I find out all the routes in the city, and who has what territory?"

"You dig," said Donnelly, giving him a faintly sympathetic smile, "and if you find yourself up against the same people who made trouble two years ago you be damned sure to carry your gun."

This was not reassuring but on the other hand it seemed infinitely remote as a possibility. Pruden returned to his office and began digging for facts, his work made easier by Maria Ardizzone's mention of the name Materas. He found it in the yellow pages: Joseph and Alice Materas, Jack Frost Ice Cream distributors, warehouse at 100 First Street, offices at 105 First Street. He was about to call them when the telephone rang at his desk: it was Madame Karitska.

"I am glad to find you," she told him. "Madame Souffrant is just beginning the voodoo ceremony and I have gained permission to watch, and for you also. This is very unusual. If you are to become Commissar of Police one day—"

He grinned. "If? I thought you were sure."

"—then this would be very good for you to see," she concluded. "We have taken Luis Mendez by taxi to 110 Third Street, to a building just behind Madame Souffrant's apartment house at 108."

Pruden considered the Materas, and he considered the voodoo ceremony, and he realized that knowing Madame Karitska was having its effect upon him: he really was curious. "I'll be there in ten minutes," he told her, and hung up.

"Where do I tell the Chief you're going?" asked Benson at the switchboard as Pruden hurried past him.

Pruden smiled. "Tell him I'm on my way to see a voodoo ceremony," he said, and was more than rewarded by the look on Benson's face.

Chapter 9

Madame Karitska met him in the alleyway next to 108 Third Street. "It's begun," she told him, "so we must walk and speak very quietly. Madame Souffrant examined Luis and confirmed that three spirits of the dead have been sent after him and that his soul has already been given to the lord of the cemetery."

"Good God, and you believe this?" he said, his brows slanting incredulously.

She brushed this aside impatiently. "What does it matter what you or I believe? It is Luis who believes." She regarded him with exasperation. "It has been very tiring trying to find a banana tree and we have had to substitute a young willow tree instead. You think it is easy looking for a banana tree in Trafton? Also it is seven o'clock and I'm hungry. Madame Souffrant is confident, however, because her cult is very similar to Luis'."

"That's good. Where the hell are we?"

"At the *oum'phor,* or temple as you might call it. Shall we go in now?"

He followed her down the alley into the rear, where a high board fence had been erected around a dilapidated old garage. The yard inside the fence was grassless and contained what looked to be junk: stones, jugs, lamps, and innumerable drawings made in chalk or lime on the hard-beaten earth. Madame Karitska led him through a small gate at the side and they tiptoed inside the garage.

Here Luis Mendez had been laid out on the earth floor beside an intricately decorated vertical pole; he had been stripped of everything but white shorts. All kinds of delicate white designs had been drawn on the earth around him. His head was wrapped in a bandage that ran from the top of his head to his jaw, and a second bandage bound his two big toes together. His eyes were open but vacant. The garage was dark except for candles burning at various points beside Luis' body and several lanterns hanging on the wall. The air was thick with incense. Half a dozen people surrounded Madame Souffrant, who was intoning, "In the name of God the Father, God the Son, and God the Holy Ghost, in the name of Mary, in the name of Jesus, in the name of all the saints, all the dead . . ."

A strange and eerie chill rose at the nape of Pruden's neck and traveled across his scalp. That stern and declamatory voice rose and fell like a bird in the hushed and darkened room, like a hawk or an eagle, he thought, beating its wings against the walls until the walls appeared to recede, disappearing altogether, and he stood in astonishment, centuries removed from Trafton, listening to a priestess speak to the gods.

When the incantations abruptly ended he felt disoriented and confused; he discovered he was sweating profusely for reasons he couldn't understand and which his rational mind could not explain. He stole a glance at Madame Karitska and saw that her eyes were closed and her face serene. As the rituals continued he returned his attention to Madame Souffrant, but if what followed seemed to him bizarre and preposterous he didn't smile; he was unable to forget what he had felt during the incantations, unable to forget a sense of Presences, of forces appealed to and converging. . . .

Luis Mendez lay like a corpse except for an occasional twitching or shouting of what sounded like obscenities. As Pruden watched, small piles of corn and peanuts and pieces of bread were distributed at certain points of his body, and just as he wondered why in hell somebody's leftover breakfast was being heaped on Luis, two hens and a rooster were carried into the *oum'phor* and given to Madame Souffrant. She grasped the chickens, one under each arm, and held them low over Luis so that they could peck at the food on his body while at the same time she began a curious crossing and uncrossing of Luis' arms, chanting *"Ente, te, te, tete, te . . ."* When the piles of corn had been reduced in size the chickens were exchanged for the rooster, and Pruden felt a stab of alarm. The angry cock left small, bloody wounds as it moved up Luis' body, heading for his face: barely in time someone stepped forward to cover the man's eyes. After this the cock was carried away and turned loose in the yard outside, and lighted candles began to be passed over Luis from head to foot, again weaving that same strange pattern while the incantations of *Ente, te, te, tete* rose in volume.

Abruptly Madame Souffrant became silent, moved to a basin, gathered up liquid in cupped hands, and vigorously slapped Luis' face. Others moved in and began to thrash Luis with water; he was helped to a half-sitting position and whipped with small, dripping wet sacks until the bandages fell away from his dripping body. Cloves of garlic were thrust into his mouth while Madame Souffrant continued to call on the dead spirits to depart, her voice rising to a crescendo.

Suddenly Luis shuddered violently from head to foot and fell back on the earth almost unconscious.

Madame Souffrant ceased her incantations and leaned over him. "Luis," she called. "Luis Mendez. Luis, is it you?"

"Yes," he said in a calm and normal voice.

"I think the dead spirits are leaving now," whispered Madame Karitska, her eyes bright and intent.

A jar filled with something alcoholic was poured over a stone lying in a dish, and flames sprang up. The steaming dish was carried to Luis and passed over his body, again describing that same intricate pattern of movement, after which Madame Souffrant put it down, seized a bottle of fluid, lifted it to her lips, drank from it several times, and each time spat it through her teeth over Luis.

"We move out into the yard now," said Madame Karitska in a low voice, nudging Pruden, and he followed her and the others outside to a corner of the enclosure where a deep hole had been dug. To Pruden's surprise it had grown dark while they were inside, and the lamps encircling the hole sent bizarre shadows flickering up and down the fence. He turned to see Luis limp from the building on the arms of two young men, and as Luis approached the illuminated circle, Pruden saw that he looked stronger, his eyes wide open and no longer clouded. He was carefully helped down into the hole and a tree of equal stature was placed in it beside him. The rooster, protesting, was again passed over Luis' body and the incantations begun again, concluding at last with Madame Souffrant calling out in a ringing, down-to-earth voice, "I demand that you return the life of this man. . . . I, Souffrant, demand the life of this man. I buy for cash—I pay you—I owe nothing!"

With this she grasped a jug, poured its contents over Luis' head, broke it with a blow of her fist and let the pieces fall into the hole. She was still chanting as Luis was pulled out of the hole. The rooster was placed inside it instead, and buried alive at the foot of the tree.

The ritual was not over yet but Pruden's gaze was fixed on Luis now, who was being helped into a long white gown. He stood unsupported; his skin had color again and his eyes were bright, no longer haunted. It was unbelievable when Pruden remembered the prostrate, gray-faced, nearly lifeless man he'd seen lying on the earth only a little while ago.

"He will remain here now near the sacred peristyle for several days," said Madame Karitska briskly. "If the tree dies, Luis will live. If the tree lives, Luis will die. Only when this is known will he leave, dead or alive."

"Yes," said Pruden, still bemused.

"Are you all right?" she asked sharply.

He pulled himself together with an effort. "Of course I'm all right. We can leave now?"

She nodded, and they walked back to his car. As they drove away he said, "Okay, explain."

"Madame Souffrant would be the better person to ask," she pointed out. "I can only tell you what she discovered when she visited Luis in his room. She is, you know, a detective in her own way."

"Oh?" His voice was sardonic.

"She found what she called a 'disaster lamp' buried in the Malone back yard," continued Madame Karitska. "We went out, all of us, and in a corner of the yard under a tree it was obvious that digging had taken place within the last week." Madame Karitska added distastefully, "I must say the lamp was a disaster in itself when we dug it up. It smelled terribly. Madame Souffrant said it contained the gall bladder of an ox, soot, lime juice, and castor oil."

"All right, but how would Luis know it was there?" demanded Pruden.

"Exactly," said Madame Karitska. "Someone obviously had to tell him it was there, or add to it some other type of symbol that was terrifying to Luis. Madame Souffrant's guess was that graveyard dust was sent him through the mail, or left on his doorstep. It would have to be someone who knew he was a believer. In any case Luis felt he was doomed and that the gods of the cemetery had taken him."

"Well, I can't say it's nonsense any longer," Pruden admitted. "I saw how ill he was, and I saw his resurrection."

Madame Karitska said quietly, "When one believes

—what is this, after all, but the demonic side of faith?"

Already the memory of the *oum'phor* was receding, releasing him from its spell so that Pruden said almost angrily, "It goes against everything believable, a man dooming himself to die."

Madame Karitska said dryly, "Yet you are witnessing precisely this. You forget that everything that makes a person human is invisible: his thoughts, his emotions, his soul. You forget that electricity is invisible, too, and can kill."

"Okay—the invisible can kill. *Maybe.*" He pulled up in front of her apartment and opened the door for her. "It's late."

She nodded. "Nearly midnight," she said with a sigh. "I left a sign on my door saying that I would be back at twelve and—*voilà*—I am back at twelve. But not the right twelve," she added, "and I shall wonder how many clients I lost today."

"Well," Pruden told her with a faint smile, "if you find your cupboard bare, give me a call and I'll take you to dinner. But a very quick one," he added, "because I'm probably losing my mind but tomorrow I plan to begin looking for someone who wants the Mendez brothers out of the way."

"Thank you," she said simply, and he watched her walk up the steps to her apartment looking as regal and grand as if she were returning from the opera.

In the morning his early call reached Mrs. Materas, the wife of the distributor. Her husband had the flu, she said, but they worked together and she knew everything that he did. She would be glad to meet him at the office if he didn't mind waiting until she'd gone to church: the church was only two blocks from their office.

Pruden was there at twelve-thirty, and he sat down with Mrs. Materas and proceeded to learn rather a lot about the ice-cream-truck business, and Jack Frost in particular. The parent company, Mrs. Materas explained, was in Rosewood Heights, New Jersey, with franchised distributors in thirty-five states. Her husband had been a vendor for years but had bought his franchise fourteen years ago. It was a good business. "Hectic but good," she said. "We have ninety-four Jack Frost trucks working Trafton. They keep the trucks in our garages down the street, and we sell them all the ingredients as well as napkins, cones, paper cups, and plastic spoons. We also help them finance their trucks."

"Any trouble lately on the routes?" Pruden asked.

"Oh no," she said, "we've never had any trouble. I know a couple of other companies had difficulties a few years ago but we've never had any."

"Any of your trucks move in the Dell section?"

She shook her head. "That's Mr. Freezee territory. Our trucks operate only in the city proper."

"Who decides all this?" he asked with interest.

She laughed. "Whoever gets there first, that's who. We happened to be first in the city, that's all, and never got around to expanding into the Dell section. Here, I'll show you." She walked over to the open door, closed it and showed him a map thumbtacked to the wall. "As you can see—"

Pruden walked over and looked at the map. The Jack Frost territories were colored in pink, the competition routes in green. He said, "The green areas, what companies have those routes?"

"Mr. Freezee."

"I thought you said Mr. Freezee had only the Dell section?"

"Oh, they started there," Mrs. Materas explained, "but over the past several years they've been expanding. Buying out other suburban territories here and there."

"For cash?"

Mrs. Materas shrugged. "I really couldn't tell you. Some of those small independents often run into debt the first year and sell out cheap."

Pruden nodded, his face thoughtful. He wondered whether Mrs. Materas had noticed lately that Jack Frost was now completely encircled by Mr. Freezee; almost, he thought, like a noose. "Well, thanks," he said. "I appreciate your help. One other question: have you many Puerto Rican drivers?"

She thought a moment. "A fair number, maybe 30 per cent. They're good workers. Ambitious. You can't explain why—?"

"Not yet," he said with a friendly smile, "but one day I will."

He went next to see Maria Ardizzone again, because he was remembering her hesitation when he'd asked if anything in particular had upset Luis just before he became ill. It had been a very slight hesitation but he'd caught it and he decided it was time to find out whether it meant anything. When he looked up her home address he found that she lived at Mrs. Malone's boardinghouse, which explained how she and Luis had met when the Mendez brothers worked such long hours.

Her room was smaller than his, and at the top of the house, and hot. It was the sort of room that he might have expected if he'd sat down first to consider her character: she had taken it ambitiously in hand, as she would Luis if he lived, and she had painted and slip-covered and decorated until it looked like one of those magazine photo stories captioned "Turning-an-Attic-Room-into-an-Apartment." There was a great deal of white shag everywhere and black-and-white flowered cloth, and fat red pillows, and little glass-topped tables. Pruden, who liked to see the bones of a room—bare floors and furniture—thought it rather suffocating but he admitted that it was as pretty as Maria.

He found her upset. "I just don't understand about this voodoo business. Luis went with me to church every Sunday," she complained in a worried voice. "I'm a Roman Catholic and he said he was too. He never mentioned any—any *voodoo* cults."

He agreed that it could be rather a shock.

"And then to hear—I can't even see him," she protested, looking suddenly very young.

"He was better last night. I saw him."

"But *I* wanted to make him better," she said simply. "I was praying hard for him."

"Then I think your prayers must have—well, brought him the people who *could* help. Do you still want to help him?"

Her eyes widened. "But of course! Oh, you mustn't think it's made any difference. It's just I don't understand why he didn't tell me."

Pruden said gently, "He might have felt a little

embarrassed, you know, or thought he'd lose you. You're not Puerto Rican, are you?"

She thought about this and appeared to appreciate it. "That's true."

"So let's get down to facts." Pruden seated himself in a chair that brought his knees almost to his chin, got up and moved to the couch, which placed a more sustaining weight under him. "You hesitated when I asked if Luis had been upset by anything before he became sick."

"Oh, that," sniffed Maria. "Such a small thing, and yet—and yet you know it was the only time I've ever seen him look—well, so *changed*. Arturo's death made him sad—he cried, you know, but this—"

"Tell me."

She nodded. "It was the day after Arturo's burial and Luis had only just gone back to work. I came downstairs—we were going to go for a walk—and I saw a man on the stairs below me. Luis was standing in the door of his room watching the man leave and he had this funny look on his face, as if he'd been hit in the stomach. For about ten minutes after that he wasn't himself—very quiet, not listening—and then we went out to a movie and after that he was fine."

"Had the man been in Luis' room?"

"Yes, but Luis didn't say why. I thought it must have been a friend of Arturo's come to pay his respects."

"You don't know who the man was?"

Maria shook her head.

"Could you describe him?"

"Oh no," she said, "I saw only his back. Maybe Mrs. Malone saw him, though. She's very fussy about keeping the front door locked. Everybody has to ring the bell if they don't have a key."

"I'll go down and ask," he said, and thanked her.

Mrs. Malone, unearthed in the kitchen, wiped her hands on her apron and thought about Pruden's question. "Someone to see Luis . . ." she repeated gravely. "Well, I can't think who that would be, since Luis didn't get callers, if you know what I mean." Her brow suddenly lifted. "Oh yes, I remember. A young man, right after dinner. Asked me to tell Luis that Carlos wanted to see him. Yes, that was his name, Carlos. . . . I told him I was busy and he'd have to find Luis himself, second floor front."

"Do you remember what he looked like?"

Mrs. Malone closed her eyes. "Black hair and mustache. Good-looking young man, twenty-five or twenty-six. What I'd call a sharp dresser. Bright colors. Sharp."

"What sort of mustache?"

"Oh, the dashing kind. You know what they're wearing these days."

Pruden nodded and wrote it down. "Thanks, Mrs. Malone," he said, and went out to telephone Bill Kane, who was off duty today but had patrolled Fifth Street for three years and might recognize the description. He read it to Kane over the phone.

"Sounds like Carlos Torres," Kane said cautiously. "Hangs out a lot at the Caballeros Social Club."

This was better luck than Pruden had expected. "Any visible means of employment?"

Kane sighed into the telephone. "I don't really know, Lieutenant. At least he's never done anything antisocial, to my knowledge. Knows a lot of people. Could be a bookie, I suppose, but frankly I've never seen him up to anything suspicious. Gets around a lot, now that you mention it. Nice, polite, bright-eyed guy. Neat and sociable."

"Mmmm," murmured Pruden, and decided he would ask for a tail on Mr. Carlos Torres just to see where his getting around took him.

Twenty-four hours later, by Monday night, Pruden had a neat list on what Carlos Torres had done with his Sabbath evening and with the first day of the new week. It was an interesting list: Kane was right, the young man got around. His tail had picked him up at four-thirty on Sunday when he was walking with a girl named Esperita. He'd returned the girl to her house and stopped at the Hy-Grade Laundry, where overtime was going on in the rear section. He'd had dinner at the Grand Hotel, a decent place on Seventh Street where he lived in a rented room on the ground floor. While he'd been eating a man had stopped to talk to him for fifteen minutes, followed by another, who had coffee with him. Then Carlos had picked up another girl—a blonde this time named Carol—and had taken her to a movie. After that he'd strolled up to a shop at 1023 Broad Street, gone down an alley next to the shop, knocked on a door and gone inside. One hour later he returned to his hotel. His lights had gone out at midnight.

In the morning he'd taken the subway to the Dell section, where he'd gone to a business building and entered the offices of one Harold Robichaud, Amusement Enterprises, Inc. He'd then gone on to the office of a John Tortorelli, attorney-at-law, also in the Dell section, and at noon was back at 1023 Broad Street again, this time entering the shop (The Bazaar Curio Shop, Everything Bizarre) by the front door. After another visit to Hy-Grade Laundry he was now at the Caballeros Social Club again, this time with a redhead named Marcia.

Bookie? thought Pruden. Messenger? Go-between? Wheeler-dealer? The name of Tortorelli was vaguely familiar. He asked for a run-down on Harold Robichaud and John Tortorelli and decided to pay a visit to 1023 Broad Street, which was one item on the list he could check out immediately.

He found the Bazaar Curio Shop a shabby but perfectly respectable little shop; in fact he'd noticed it a number of times in passing because of the carved masks displayed in a window. One window held rather good-quality secondhand books—Pruden guessed that this had been the shop's original purpose—while the right-hand window contained masks and figurines as well as a small assortment of necklaces and rings from Africa and the Orient. Small gold-leaf letters on the door announced that R. Ramon was the proprietor.

Pruden walked inside and nodded to the man who glanced up from a ledger at the counter. There was no one else in the shop. "Good morning," said Pruden.

"Morning, sir." The voice was courteous and pleasing to the ear. "Please feel free to browse, but if there's anything you wish—" He left the rest unspoken.

As he thanked the man and turned toward the masks, Pruden gave his face a quick glance and filed it away in his memory. It was a singularly homely face, he thought, yet not a unpleasant one: wire spectacles with very thick lenses, a thin wide mouth, receding chin, and receding hairline. He looked strangely like a frog with extended, magnified eyes, and in some odd way he appeared very much at home among the bizarre and the exotic, like a highly glazed, porcelain gargoyle set down among the other oddities. As Pruden examined masks, his back to the counter, he could feel the man watching him. He turned and said briskly, "Have you a card? I'm completely lost among all this but I've an uncle who collects this sort of thing. He'd go mad here."

"Oh, one hopes not," said the man gently. "Yes, I've cards." He indicated a neat stack of them beside his cash register and Pruden walked over and took one. "And you're Mr. Ramon?" he asked, reading it.

"Yes."

Pruden nodded, tucked the card in his pocket, and turned toward the books, running a finger casually over their spines like a man trying to memorize titles for a nonexistent uncle. Many of them dealt with the occult but there were also musty volumes on colonial history, herbs, theology, and American Indians. With a final nod he walked out of the store, closed the door behind him and continued up the street. So much for that, he thought, and walked back to headquarters to see what might have turned up on Robichaud and Tortorelli.

He need not have worried: there was plenty, all of it very interesting indeed.

An hour later, after digesting the reports brought to him, Pruden walked into his superior's office with a puzzled frown. He said, "Look, have there been any signs lately that the Syndicate might be moving into the Puerto Rican section in Trafton?"

Startled, the Chief said, "What have you come up with?"

"Some interesting coincidences."

His superior sighed. "That's how it usually starts: whispers, echoes, rumors and coincidences. I don't know why the hell they'd want to move in on Fifth Street, though, they had a rough enough time getting into the black section. At least five of their men turned up in alleys with knives in their backs and they ended up making a deal with Bones Jackson, didn't they?"

"Maybe they learned something," said Pruden. "Maybe they're going about this in a different way, staying out and letting Puerto Ricans take over." He slipped two sheets of paper on the Chief's desk. "I had a tail put on one Carlos Torres yesterday, for reasons so microscopic it would be embarrassing to explain, but damned if he doesn't seem to be leading me into Syndicate territory. I may be wrong but I think something's up."

He sat down and watched the Chief's face and was not surprised to see it change when he reached the second paragraph. "Tortorelli! He's certainly Syndicate—their best lawyer. And Robichaud . . ." He scowled. "That name rings a bell."

Pruden nodded. "You'll find him on the next page. You remember the ice-cream-truck war in the Dell section two years ago? The original distributors lost the battle, filed for bankruptcy, and Robichaud Amusement Enterprises very kindly came along, bought them out, and took over the Mr. Freezee business there."

The Chief whistled softly. "And I see that Tortorelli handled the purchase. We suspected the Syndicate connection but this Tortorelli involvement was kept damned quiet."

Pruden nodded. "Some crusading news reporter uncovered it a year ago when doing a piece on Tortorelli."

"How does this Carlos Torres fit into this?"

Pruden hesitated. "An ice-cream vendor here in Trafton died ten days ago under strange circumstances. A Jack Frost vendor. Puerto Rican, no enemies. Now his brother, who also owns a Jack Frost ice-cream truck, isn't expected to live out the week."

The Chief's brows shot up. "But he's still alive? What does he say? You've talked to him?"

"He's—uh—unconscious," said Pruden. "However, the only person to visit him at the time was Carlos Torres, which is why I had a tail put on him."

The Chief sat back, eyes narrowed in thought. "And he visits Tortorelli and Robichaud Enterprises. . . . What about the Hy-Grade Laundry?"

"I'm asking around."

The Chief nodded. "I don't like the sound of it, frankly. You'd better turn over whatever else you're working on to Benson. Go after this full-time and let me know what you need."

"I could certainly use Swope if he's available," said Pruden.

"You've got him. Anything else?"

Pruden stood up and walked to the door and then with one hand on the knob he suddenly grinned, a sense of mischief overtaking him. "Well, I wouldn't mind hearing that a certain willow tree on Third Street —that ought to be a banana tree—has shriveled up and died." He went out, gently closing the door behind him.

Chapter 10

Leaving headquarters at five o'clock that same day, Pruden hesitated on the step and then instead of climbing into his car he turned left and began walking toward Eighth Street. He found Madame Karitska at home, with Gavin curled up on her couch with his homework.

"My dear Lieutenant," said Madame Karitska, "you look badly in need of coffee. Nothing so anemic as your American brew but something to fortify you. I will also prepare you a cucumber sandwich."

"Aren't you supposed to be at St. Bonaventure's?" Pruden asked, throwing himself into the chair opposite Gavin.

The boy grinned. "It's okay. I came over to see Madame Karitska on Saturday but she wasn't here, so the school said I could come tonight instead. Now that

I'm an orphan, you know, they give me special privileges."

"Which of course you refuse," Pruden said with a smile.

"Not if I can help it," grinned Gavin. "Have you found out who killed Arturo yet, and made Luis sick? Madame Karitska's been explaining why she wasn't here Saturday when I came."

"No, but I've been finding out a hell of a—excuse me, a heck of a lot of other things."

"Such as what, may I ask?" said Madame Karitska, returning from the kitchen with a tray.

"Well, for one thing," confessed Pruden, "I have to swallow my considerable pride and admit this isn't the small neighborhood affair I thought it would be last Saturday night. My apologies to you," he added, picking up a sandwich, "but I honestly didn't think it would amount to more than an ex-boy friend of Maria's, or a neighbor who was jealous of Arturo's success. Now it looks like the biggest case I've tackled yet. The Syndicate appears to be involved somehow."

"The Syndicate! Holy cow!" said Gavin, eyes widening. "You know about the Syndicate, don't you, Madame Karitska?"

She seated herself on the couch beside Gavin and inserted a cigarette into a long holder. "It is, I believe, very organized crime?"

"*Very* organized crime," Pruden said dryly. "And not, I might add, a group that usually dabbles in voodoo. We've been working our tails off today and it looks as if for some reason they're after the Jack Frost ice-cream business here in Trafton."

Madame Karitska laughed. "What a strange thing to be after!"

He nodded. "Both Arturo and Luis drove ice-cream trucks, remember? Here, look at the facts," he said, and brought from his pocket a condensed list of Carlos Torres' activities. Handing it to Madame Karitska he said, "Two years ago in the Dell section there was what came to be known in the media as the 'ice-cream war.' One of the vendors was kidnapped and then released, three ice-cream trucks were bombed on the streets, and the Mr. Freezee garages broken into and expensive machinery stolen or destroyed. This went on for six or eight weeks and then suddenly stopped."

"You were not told why?" asked Madame Karitska.

"No, but one looks for patterns. In this case shortly after the turbulence ended the Mr. Freezee distributorship was taken over by Harold Robichaud of Amusement Enterprises. We know nothing about him except that he bought it, but about the attorney who handled the purchase we know a great deal. His name is John Tortorelli and he's a Syndicate man."

Madame Karitska frowned. "But you are speaking of the past, of something that happened two years ago."

"Yes, but we begin to suspect the scenario is about to be repeated."

"And this Carlos Torres?" asked Madame Karitska, glancing through the memo. "Who is this Carlos Torres?"

"He paid a call on Luis twelve hours before Luis took to his bed. In fact he was the only stranger who ever paid a call on Mendez. He lives just off Fifth Street and he's Puerto Rican."

"Ah," murmured Madame Karitska. "A link—I see

. . . and he led you to these others? But this Tortorelli and Robichaud . . . do they seem to you the sort of men learned in voodoo?"

Pruden laughed. "Absolutely not, but we'll get to that eventually."

"This Carlos Torres then, perhaps he would kill by voodoo?"

"Carlos?" He shook his head. "Not likely."

Madame Karitska said with a hint of exasperation in her voice, "You are no longer investigating what has happened to the Mendez brothers, then?"

Pruden sighed. "Look, you're missing the point. This has broadened into Syndicate stuff. It's big, bigger than the Mendez brothers. It could turn into the biggest case I've uncovered."

She said gently, "On the contrary, I think *you* are missing the point, Lieutenant. You speak of patterns and scenarios and what took place two years ago but you do not see that suddenly a very original mind has become involved now. The past is *not* repeating itself. You speak of bombings and kidnappings, but someone has entered the picture who side-steps physical violence. Now there is violence against the spirit. One cannot help admire the originality, do you not agree? The perfect crime."

"You keep saying that," he said crossly, and gave her a resentful glance. He was tired and he had expected approval, even admiration; instead she insisted on returning him to Luis Mendez, who was only a link to something greater.

"You do not feel," she went on crisply, "that the mind of a man who could conceive of such a murder is infinitely more subtle, infinitely more sophisticated and dangerous than your Syndicate criminal?"

"We're only starting," he pointed out defensively. "It'll all unwind like a spool of thread. Luis is still alive, isn't he?"

"Yes," she said, "but so is the willow tree, and gives every evidence of remaining alive. Why do you believe they want the Jack Frost ice-cream business, or any ice-cream business?"

"We don't know yet but we'll find out."

"This Ramon," Madame Karitska said, glancing at the list. "You have looked into him too?"

"Oh yes. No record. Clean as a whistle," said Pruden, and was glad to have the subject changed. "I visited his shop first thing this morning."

"Yes?"

"You'd love it," he told her with a smile. "Books on the supernatural, books on haunted houses. Some spectacular hand-carved masks from Africa and South America."

"Hey, I'd love to have one of those," Gavin said eagerly. "Could you take me on Saturday, Madame Karitska? The kids would get a real bang out of something wild hanging on our dorm wall."

She smiled at him. "I will take you on Saturday, yes, but I think I may stop in there tomorrow to first make certain it is—how do you say?—okay for a young boy?"

"She's tough," Gavin said to Pruden, nodding. "She doesn't want me to know about porno and all that."

"She's not tough, she's cagey," said Pruden, finishing his coffee and standing up. "She'll walk in and check out Mr. Ramon for you, admire the ring he's wearing, ask to hold it, and tell us later what he eats every day for breakfast."

But it was not a ring that Madame Karitska succeeded in holding when she visited the Bazaar Curio Shop on Tuesday afternoon; it was a fountain pen, and it was only with considerable finesse that she managed this. When she arrived at the shop there were already several customers there, and Madame Karitska moved quietly among the books, from time to time glancing covertly at the man behind the counter. A strange little man, she thought. He gave every evidence of being amiable but she came to the conclusion that of all the masks on display in the shop, his was the most formidable. In the meantime she waited, and when the others had gone she moved toward the counter carrying a copy of Crowley's *Magick in Theory and Practice*. She had moved quietly and Ramon's back was turned. She reached for the pen he had been writing with and it was in her hand when he turned and looked at her. Their glances met and locked, and Madame Karitska found it necessary to steady herself against the counter.

He said softly, "You will put down my pen."

She placed the pen back on the counter.

"Thank you," he said and with an amused glance at the book in her hand he said, "Aleister Crowley, I see. . . . You're interested in black magic, perhaps?"

"Perhaps."

But he had lost interest, and his mask was back again. "It will be seven-fifty, please," he said.

She paid him, took the book, and walked out, her heart beating very quickly. She felt curiously drained of energy, as if recovering from a bout of fever that had left her nerves trembling and her body weak. She went at once to a telephone booth and dialed Pruden's number. When he answered she said, "Lieutenant, I think you should—I think you must—check out Mr. Ramon again."

"Is this Madame Karitska?" he said. "Your voice sounds changed. Look, I'm in the middle of a conference but if you can explain—"

A wave of nausea swept her; she dropped the receiver and stumbled outside, Pruden's voice following her through the open door. Outside she stood drawing in deep breaths of air, her hands trembling as she clung to the door for support. It was necessary for her to remain there several minutes before she felt well enough to return the receiver of the phone to its hook and to begin her walk back to Eighth Street.

Pruden found Madame Karitska's call frustrating, coming as it did in the middle of a planning session with the Chief, Swope, Benson, and a man named Callahan. He said, "Excuse me a minute," and called Madame Karitska back at her apartment, but when there was no answer he hung up and turned back to the others. "All right, tell me what you found out about the Hy-Grade Laundry," he asked Swope.

"Something very interesting."

"Let's hear it."

"Right." Swope picked up his reading glasses and put them on. "Back in November of last year there was an explosion at the laundry."

"Bomb?"

"No, the investigators traced it to a boiler, but the odd thing is that the owners sold out after it happened, and rather fast. It wasn't a bomb, it was a boiler blowing up and yet they sold."

"Sabotage?"

"It has that smell," said Swope. "A boiler doesn't need a bomb to blow it up—there are a dozen things you can do to accomplish the same thing—but in any case they sold. Now it's under new management, a family named Torres, and guess who the youngest son is."

Pruden felt a prickling of excitement. "Carlos?"

"You've just won the box of Crackerjack. And," he added, "the attorney who handled the purchase was John Tortorelli."

"Good Lord," said Pruden. "The Syndicate *is* moving in."

"Looks like it. Same pattern."

"I don't get it," said Callahan, baffled. "The Syndicate goes where the money is, and I wouldn't have thought there was anything to tempt them around Fifth Street. Of course there's crime there—gambling, drugs, prostitution, numbers—but it's all smalltime, petty. Nothing worth organizing."

"Looks like it's getting organized now," Pruden said grimly. "I take it the laundry is headquarters, and Carlos their bag man. What's the latest on him, by the way?"

The Chief handed him a sheet of paper. "Same pattern. He moves between his hotel, the laundry, Robichaud, Tortorelli, and the Caballeros Club."

"So what do we do?" asked Benson.

Pruden said, "I'd like to see Robichaud and Tortorelli placed on round-the-clock surveillance, informers rounded up and questioned, and a camera put on Hy-

Grade Laundry twenty-four hours a day."

"We've already got Jack the Lip downstairs," Benson said. "The guys thought you'd want to question him, although Jack insists he doesn't know anything about a Syndicate moving into Fifth Street."

Pruden nodded and rose. "I'll go down and see what I can get out of him. I don't," he said wearily, "think we're going to get much sleep for the next few days."

"So what else is new?" asked the Chief in a kindly voice.

It was seven o'clock before Pruden finished interviewing the handful of informants that had been brought in, and the only thing he'd learned was that an icecream vendor out in the northern section of Trafton had been taken ill and was dying. He was a Jack Frost man, and his name was Raphael Alvarez, and he was six months out of Puerto Rico. "Enough to give a guy the whammies," the informant said with a shiver. "Just says he's going to die and lies there."

Like Luis, he thought. . . . It reminded Pruden of Luis and then of Madame Karitska's aborted phone call during the afternoon. She'd said Ramon ought to be checked again—that much he'd heard, and then they'd been cut off before she could explain why. He stood on the steps at headquarters debating whether to eat, grab a few hours' sleep, or visit the Bazaar Shop.

Swope, coming up behind him, said, "Where you off to now, Lieutenant?"

Pruden made his decision. "I think I'll just take a look at the Bazaar Shop again. Look around a bit. Care to come along?"

"Why not?" said Swope affably, falling into step

beside him as he began walking. "I told the wife she wouldn't be seeing much of me for a few days. Place is closed, though, isn't it?"

Pruden nodded. "Yes, but on Sunday night it was closed and Torres went around to the back. I thought—"

"I dig," said Swope. "How much further?"

"Next block, on the left."

As they neared the store a small truck passed them and slowed down, signaling a turn to the left. Its sides were painted bright scarlet; in gold carousel script were printed the words BAZAAR CURIO SHOP—Everything Bizarre—1023 Broad Street, R. Ramon, Prop. The van turned into the alleyway beside the shop and disappeared.

"Not altogether closed," pointed out Swope.

"No," said Pruden.

Crossing the street they reached the alley in time to see the scarlet truck park in the dilapidated garage at the end of the driveway. Two young men climbed out, picked up their caps and lunch boxes and began walking down the alley toward the street. "Hey," one of them said sharply, turning and pointing, and his companion hurried back to the garage and swung the doors closed; then they continued out to Broad Street, passing Pruden and Swope, and walked up the street and turned the corner.

"They didn't lock those doors. I wouldn't mind taking a look inside," Pruden said hopefully.

"It does seem like a gift from heaven," agreed Swope. "Let's go."

The layout of the building was surprisingly simple: it had once been an old house to which the shop had been added in the front. The rear contained a yard, a side porch, a garage, and all the accouterments of a conventional frame house, including an ancient apple tree. No lights shone in the windows; the place looked deserted. They very casually swung open one unlocked garage door and slipped inside.

Swope, testing the back doors of the van, said, "Locked."

Pruden peered into the front seat of the truck. There was a bunk behind the driver's seat for sleeping on long trips, but the wall behind it was windowless and seemed to be solid, with no point of entry into the storage behind it. He decided to climb inside and make certain of this, and had one foot on the floor of the garage and the other in the cab of the truck when he lost his balance and fell against the door.

Behind him he heard Swope exclaim, "What the hell!"

Pruden, looking down, realized to his astonishment that the floor of the garage was moving. He regained his balance, looked for Swope, and found him several feet above him: the garage doors were suddenly at a level with his waist as the floor slowly descended like an elevator. Swope had jumped clear and was standing in the doorway. He shouted, "For God's sake jump, Lieutenant!"

Pruden stood paralyzed, wanting to run, wanting to join Swope, but wanting also to see what the hell lay below him. A moment later his decision was made for him as the threshold of the garage doors passed out of sight. Pruden turned back to the door of the van, climbed inside and crawled up on the sleeping shelf. There were several blankets piled in one end: he curled up in a corner and drew the blankets over him.

The descent of the truck slowed, and he and the truck emerged into a lighted room below. He heard a low murmur of voices and the clink of keys unlocking the rear of the van. Two men jumped inside; he could hear the hollow sound of their feet walking around a few feet away from him, separated only by the wall against which he lay. A dolly was wheeled up, objects began being unloaded, and then came a new sound: a hammering on the sides of the truck.

"Okay, Carlos, bring the Freezee signs," a man shouted, and the sides of the truck were assaulted again. Pruden kept himself small and quiet as he drew certain conclusions: Carlos Torres was here, and signs were being switched. An old hijacking trick, he reflected, but what did it mean? They'd mentioned Freezee signs. Presumably the Bazaar Shop truck would drive away as a Mr. Freezee delivery truck, but why, and with what?

A loud, irritating buzzer interrupted the hammering.

"Trouble at the back door," a man called sharply, and Pruden heard footsteps racing away into the distance, echoing as if in a hall of some kind. After listening for a minute he concluded that he was the only person left in the garage. He crawled gingerly down from the bunk and stuck his head out of the door and looked around him. He was in a very neat underground cement-walled room with an exit that led up a long ramp-like hall, dimly lighted, to three doors at the end. He guessed that the ramp connected with the basement of Ramon's house and shop.

Stealthily Pruden emerged and crept around to one side of the truck: it was still a blaze of scarlet, with

BAZAAR CURIO SHOP emblazoned on it in gold. He
walked around to the other side and was met with a
blue panel and jagged white letters that read MR.
FREEZEE. Neat, he thought, very neat. He moved
around to the back of the truck and bent over the
cartons that had been removed from the van and were
stacked on the dolly. Drawing out his penknife he
slit open the top of one and looked inside.

The box held Mr. Freezee popsicles.

He thought it damned careless of them to abandon
the load here when ice cream melted so fast, and then
he realized there was no dry ice anywhere in sight.
He looked into the interior of the truck and ran a hand
over its walls: this was not a refrigerated truck, and
there was no sign of ice here, either. He went back to
the carton and drew out a popsicle, pulled aside its
blue-and-white wrapping, and examined it. It gave every
evidence of being a coconut-cherry popsicle: it was red,
and it was flecked with shreds of white, but it was
warm to the touch, not cold. He tapped it with a finger;
it was plastic.

A plastic popsicle . . . Carefully he knocked it against
the side of the dolly and then slipped the wooden stick
out of the plastic rectangle. The interior was a honey-
comb of thin plastic: in the very center he found a
cellophane envelope filled with white powder. He removed it. Tearing aside the cellophane he sniffed the
white substance and then wet his finger and placed a
few grains on his tongue. It was heroin, no doubt
about it.

He thought he'd seen everything during his years on
the force but the enormity of this numbed him. It
seemed the ultimate insolence, selling drugs on the

street from innocent ice-cream trucks, those Pied Pipers of the neighborhood that brought music, bells, and laughter with them on hot mucky days, the one touch of innocence left to kids. The crowds would gather, real ice cream would be exchanged for coins and then a guy with the right password, the right gesture would get this . . . this obscenity.

It filled him with a manic fury. He thought that if Carlos and his friends came back now he would delight in taking them apart one by one. At the same time all his instincts told him to leave now, look for the right switches to the hydraulic lift, crawl into the truck and ride back upstairs into the world again. But he didn't feel wise, he felt incensed and murderous. He looked at the three doors at the far end of the ramp and then he began running up the ramp toward them, not caring whether he was seen or heard. Two of the doors had small windows in them. Through the center door he saw steps leading to the upper floor; behind the left door lay a storage and workshop room with cartons of masks and a carpenter's bench. The door on his right had no windows; he opened it and walked inside.

He had entered some kind of office or study: Ramon's, he decided, because it looked like him. The walls were hung with maps and charts—astrology charts, he guessed—and fierce-looking masks. The center of the room was occupied by a huge desk covered with drawings and diagrams. A small click-click sound troubled him until he moved to the desk and saw that beside it stood a teletype machine. Ramon certainly did himself well, he thought. A second machine in the corner caught his eye and he walked over and discovered it was a computer, an honest-to-God king-sized computer with winking lights.

Then he saw the map of Trafton on the wall behind the computer, a map with every street and alley rendered in detail, and he felt a small chill. In this room incalculable plans were being made for Trafton; he'd stumbled across some kind of command post where something was being plotted and organized for his city. He went back to the desk and studied the papers and charts on its surface. Horoscopes, he saw, staring at a thick sheaf of papers with houses of the zodiac marked off. Beside these lay a pack of tarot cards and over here . . . he peered closer. A list of typed names: Arturo Mendez, Luis Mendez, Raphael Alvarez . . . He remembered that Alvarez was the name his informant had mentioned tonight. The list was long, and Arturo's name at the top had been crossed off with red ink.

Pruden stood and thought about this. Madame Karitska had said "an original mind," and now he understood at last what she had meant. For the first time he accepted the fact that Arturo Mendez had actually been murdered and that Luis Mendez was in the process of being murdered. Not a finger had been laid on them, but here in this room a man had so clearly understood them and so accurately appraised their fears that he could manipulate their deaths without knowing anything but their history and their culture, and without ever meeting them.

"Clever," he thought, but he knew this word only concealed his unease. It was the potential behind it that disturbed him, it was the troubling sense that if this could happen to two happy, uncomplicated men, then possibly one day in the future it could reach out to him and to others.

He was lost in these thoughts when a voice spoke nearby, a voice oddly calm and almost tender. "Good evening. You realize of course, sir, that you are trespassing?"

Pruden swung around to see Ramon standing in the doorway; he had entered without a sound and stood smiling at him.

"Yes," said Pruden.

"I should, of course, be indignant or alarmed but I never waste energy on unnecessary emotion," Ramon said, the soft light glittering across the lenses of his glasses and rendering them opaque. "And I'm sure you have some suitable explanation." Was there a touch of irony in his voice? "In the meantime I'm certain we can find some practical and pragmatic solution to this confrontation if we use judgment and frankness. I've seen you before, haven't I? You were in my shop yesterday."

Pruden nodded.

"And now you are seeing what I like to think is a modern alchemist's laboratory."

The important thing, Pruden realized, was to stall for time. Swope would know what to do, Swope had seen him disappear, and thank God he'd not come alone. Calls would be going out, patrol cars rerouted, a strategy plotted. *Don't rock the boat*, he told himself, *keep it light, keep him talking.* "You're a student of the occult, I see."

Ramon laughed. "A master. How do you like my little study?"

"A bit weird," Pruden acknowledged. "Unusual, certainly." He could feel Ramon's eyes on him and it was an uncomfortable feeling because he couldn't see the man's eyes and this was even more disquieting.

"I may inquire your name, sir?" Such a gentle voice!

"Pruden."

"Ah yes. Actually, Mr. Pruden, I am a scholar and inventor. At the moment I am consultant to a group that is very interested in my research, which is highly specialized, and they are willing to pay me astronomic sums for certain research studies I've done. Absurd, of course, but I have an IQ of over two hundred, which more than makes up for the fact that I am small, almost deformed in appearance, and nearly blind." He said this softly, his eyes rooted on Pruden as he waited for his response.

"Oh?" said Pruden equally softly, and asked in a neutral voice, "And do you use your—er—research—for good or evil?"

Ramon chuckled. "A conventional question, Mr. Pruden. Power is so often used for evil, is it not? I believe it was Lord Acton who said, 'Power tends to corrupt, and absolute power corrupts absolutely.' "

"What kind of power?" asked Pruden, and decided that he must stop thinking of Swope because he had the uncanny feeling that those opaque eyes could read his mind.

"Power to destroy people." Ramon chuckled. "I could destroy you, Mr. Pruden, very easily, in less than two days. Consider that a compliment, by the way, because most people I could reduce to nothingness in hours, without violence."

"Forgive me if I'm skeptical," Pruden said.

"Oh, I can assure you it's quite possible, and entirely without physical violence of any kind. Every human being has his Achilles' heel psychologically, you see, his own self-image that he nurtures. It would take a little time to discover yours, Mr. Pruden, but you have one. Everyone does. Disturb that image, which is like the skin of a balloon, and following the loud bang there is—why, nothing at all. Or madness," he conceded modestly.

"You use drugs, of course," Pruden said harshly.

Ramon looked shocked. "My dear sir, you miss the point entirely. Of course not. You are a completely conditioned animal, Mr. Pruden, composed of habit, other people's valuations, other people's ideas, opinions, and reactions. What do you have that is yours, untouched by others? Very little. It is more likely that you have no center at all. Human beings are eternally fragmented and highly susceptible to a breakdown of the ego. Statistically, my dear sir, only one man in twenty is a leader, with the capabilities and strengths of a leader. The rest are sheep. The Chinese know this. The North Koreans discovered it for themselves when they brainwashed their captives in the fifties. Destroy that one man and the others prove no problem at all. Almost all human beings are machines, Mr. Pruden. Sleepwalkers without consciousness."

"Sleepwalkers," repeated Pruden, recognizing the phrase.

"But I think we waste time talking here," Ramon confessed with a benevolent smile. "Frankly, a small conference becomes necessary with my employees while we discuss how to solve this unexpected situation. I have never," he added with a disarming smile, "entertained a trespasser before."

"I suppose not," said Pruden.

"I would suggest that you wait in the next room while I discuss this with them. If you would be so kind—"

Pruden shrugged. "I don't mind."

"Good. The door is behind that scarlet curtain over there. You'll find cigarettes there, and a small bar. It's my living room—I can assure you I am quite civilized." Ramon walked to the curtain and drew it aside, exposing an oak door. He opened it, and flicked on the lights. "There is no trickery here, as you can see. We will keep this very brief, Mr. Pruden, with as little suspense for you as possible."

"Yes," said Pruden politely, and wondered if in passing Ramon he could get close enough to reach him but he discovered that the idea of grappling with the man filled him with ennui. He felt curiously tired, sapped of his usual energy. Anyway it had to be time for Swope, he thought. Surely now, surely any minute?

He entered a large room furnished with low couches and tables. There were no windows; instead the walls were hung with soft antique tapestries and fabric, while in the very center of the room a massive Buddha sat smiling down at him. On shelves to his right, behind glass, he saw Chinese porcelains and pieces of jade that could easily have come from a museum. It was all amazing, he thought, a sybaritic underground pied-à-terre. The theme of the room was oriental, soothing and unusual, the motif established by the Buddha, which was taller than he was, carved out of wood—teak, he realized, approaching it with curiosity—and colored with dabs of blue and red.

Abruptly he stopped, thinking *Buddha*.

Blue and red Buddha.

Madame Karitska . . . Buddha . . . danger from behind . . .

Pruden whirled just as Ramon fired the gun with a look of hatred and contempt distorting his face. The bullet caught Pruden sideways, he felt a stab of pain radiating through his chest, intense, grinding, unbearable pain and then he slumped to the floor and darkness crashed over him in waves.

Hours, days, weeks later Pruden opened his eyes to a bright ceiling and a feeling of dull uneasy discomfort. Slowly his eyes focused on a bouquet of yellow flowers and he thought, Somewhere between then and now I died. Beyond the flowers he saw a face that struck him as comical but also vaguely familiar: a deeply tanned face with a bristling white mustache and vivid blue eyes. The face rose and drifted nearer. "You're awake," it said. "I'll call the nurse."

"Who," began Pruden.

"Faber-Jones," the voice said. "We've been taking turns sitting with you, Madame Karitska and I."

"Karitska," repeated Pruden, and then as it all came back he said, "There was a Buddha. Tell her there was a Buddha."

"Right," said the voice, and vanished.

"A Buddha," Pruden told the nurse when she appeared in starched white cap. "There was a Buddha."

"Yes, Lieutenant, but take these capsules now. . . . You've been very, very ill, we nearly lost you."

When he swam back to consciousness again the ceiling was dark and the room was in shadow except for one light on a table. Next to the table sat Swope, wearing a rakish white hat.

"Yes, it's me, Lieutenant," Swope said, looking up from a magazine.

"What the hell," said Pruden, staring, "Hat?"

"Hat! This is no hat, it's a bandage," Swope growled. I just got out of the hospital five days ago and I've got to wear this damn thing until Friday when the last stitches come out. We've both been out of action, Lieutenant, but you gave us a real scare. You've been here two weeks."

This galvanized Pruden. *"How* long?"

"Surgery," Swope said, nodding. "Bullet near your heart. Top man in the country took you apart and put you together again. A quarter of an inch closer and it would have been curtains."

Pruden frowned. "It was in the popsicles," he said abruptly.

Swope nodded. "If you're able to remember how it started I'll tell you how it ended. After you disappeared down that elevator I phoned in a ten-thirteen to head-quarters and ran back to find you, except they were waiting for me. Damn near killed me, too. I was unconscious when the Chief got there so it took a while for them to realize you were in trouble too, and then they had to get a search warrant. That's what slowed things up. You don't have to worry about the popsicles, though, they made a clean sweep. The drugs came up from South America in the masks Ramon sold. Came in by truck, went out in popsicles."

A nurse came in and stopped Swope from saying any more. "We don't want to tire him now, do we?"

Pruden loathed her cheerful voice but was neverthe-less grateful and immediately fell asleep. When he awoke again his head was clear for the first time and he felt almost himself again. It was late morning, and in the chair beside his bed sat Madame Karitska.

"Well," he said, looking at her.

"Well," she returned, her eyes twinkling at him. "You are quite a hero, Lieutenant, I actually went out and bought newspapers to read about you."

"I met your Buddha, too, you know."

"So Mr. Faber-Jones told me yesterday," she said, nodding. "I am not surprised. That Mr. Ramon——" She shook her head. "Sometime when you are better I shall tell you what I saw in him. Never," she said simply, "have I felt such evil in a man, or encountered such power, such brilliance or such a twisted soul."

"He was like you," Pruden said in a wondering voice. "I mean, he spoke of the same things you do but he had it all twisted, he'd turned it upside down. He *knew*."

"Knew?"

Pruden shivered. "Motives. Weaknesses. People. Most of all people, I think. How to bend and destroy them."

"Satanic," said Madame Karitska, nodding, "but let us not speak of him today, for the sun is shining and you are alive and I have good news for you."

"Good. What is it?"

"The willow tree has died," she said. "It died quite suddenly the morning after you were shot, and Luis is back at work driving his ice-cream truck. As a matter of fact he plans one day to come in personally to thank you, and for this he is learning a speech in English."

"Well, now," he said, pleased, "I'm certainly glad to hear that. In fact if you——" But Pruden's eyes had wandered to the window and he was abruptly silent.

Someone had moved the yellow flowers to the window sill, where they were capturing the morning's brilliant sunshine in their petals and creating a blaze of gold. He thought he had never seen such color in his life, nor really looked at a flower before, and he could feel tears rising to his eyes at the impact of their beauty. A simple bouquet of daffodils in a white pottery vase . . . He had always assumed white was colorless but in the snow-like pottery he could trace reflections of yellow, and one tender blue shadow that exactly matched the blue of the sky beyond the flowers. "My God," he said in astonishment, "I'm alive. I don't think I ever understood before what it means."

"Ah," said Madame Karitska.

"Those flowers. Did you notice them, do you see the sun in them?"

"Tell me," she said, watching him closely.

"They're alive, too, in the most incredible—" He stopped, his voice unsteady. "I sound like a nut."

She shook her head. Very softly she said, "I think the patterns in the kaleidoscope have shifted a little for you, my dear Lieutenant. You have heard the expression that to nearly lose your life is to find it? You will be changed, perhaps. Aware."

"Is that what life is?"

"It is what it *can* be," she said, "Seeing, really seeing, and then at last—at last the understanding." She rose and picked up her purse and smiled down at him. "As the French say, 'One must draw back in order to leap the better.' My French grows rusty, how do they phrase it? *'Il faut reculer pour mieux sauter.'* Rest well, my friend, I will see you again tomorrow."

Chapter 11

While Lieutenant Pruden was in the hospital fighting for his life Madame Karitska and Mr. Faber-Jones became, surprisingly, rather good friends. He arrived one evening at her apartment to announce that he had grown intolerably bored with his attempts to escape clairvoyance. "My wife left me last week," he said, standing in the doorway and refusing to sit down until he had made his confession. "I'm drinking too much and I've come to realize that I'm nothing but a selfish, shallow, egotistical stuffed shirt."

"Good," said Madame Karitska promptly.

"*Good?*"

Smiling, she said, "You are suffering from a severe case of creative discontent, my dear Mr. Faber-Jones. How else do you think people can look for something new unless they become thoroughly oppressed and sated by the old? This is very promising."

"It doesn't feel promising," he said miserably. "It hurts. Can you suggest anything at all?"

"But of course," she told him. "You can begin by coming with me to the hospital to sit with Lieutenant Pruden. His father isn't well enough to go frequently and I feel someone should be with him as much as possible."

"That's *all*?"

He was so clearly disappointed in her that Madame Karitska laughed. "You would prefer something more dramatic, like work among the lepers, or giving all your money to the poor? Do not be disappointed, Mr. Faber-Jones, that too could be asked of you one day but not now, I assure you."

Faber-Jones was an eminently practical man, and for the moment a depleted one; he accepted Madame Karitska's prescription without further protest. After one visit, and learning how near death Pruden had been, he suggested with surprising humility that he take turns with Madame Karitska at the hospital. Out of the hours spent quietly at Pruden's bedside Mr. Faber-Jones received something in return: he arrived at several decisions which he put into action at once. He placed his Cavendish Square house on the market for sale, moved into a nearby apartment, and granted his wife a very generous separation allowance.

"Do you love her?" asked Madame Karitska curiously.

"Actually yes, very much," he said. "Does that sound odd from an old duffer like me? I've given her everything except myself, though, and I can't blame her for leaving. She doesn't want a divorce—she said so—and that leaves me with some hope."

"One must always have hope," Madame Karitska agreed, nodding.

"I've also decided to give a dinner party," he told her, brightening. "A new sort of dinner party, to christen my new apartment and new life. Will you come?"

"I shall look forward to it," she promised him, and on the night before Pruden was to be discharged from the hospital she presented herself at Faber-Jones' door, looking splendid in damask brocade.

He had invited four other guests, three men and a woman. Dr. Jane Tennison was a striking woman of about forty, blond and deeply tanned; she was an archaeologist, a childhood friend of Faber-Jones' and on easy terms with him. There was Peter Zoehfeld, a heavily bearded, distinguished-looking man from the United Nations. "Met him only two weeks ago," chuckled Faber-Jones. "Day I went to New York on business. We were both caught in a subway fire and stuck underground for two hours."

"Nothing," said Zoehfeld with a charming smile and a flash of dark eyes, "breaks down barriers faster than a soupçon of danger. I am delighted to meet you, Madame Karitska. My friend Mr. Faber-Jones told me I would find you a fascinating woman but he neglected to mention your beauty."

Madame Karitska gave him an amused second glance before moving on.

"And this is Dr. Berkowitz, our family medical doctor," continued Faber-Jones.

Dr. Berkowitz was a small, rather nondescript man in a baggy gray suit. His smile was genuine and warm, however, and his handshake firm; she thought he must be a very good doctor.

"And Lucas Johns," concluded Faber-Jones. "Used to be in the recording business, now he manages rock stars."

"Oh, do you handle John Painter?" asked Madame Karitska.

Mr. Johns grinned. He was perhaps fifty, with a superb mane of gray hair, very tousled, and he was wearing a fringed buckskin shirt over suede slacks. "No, but I wish I did."

"He's been tremendously helpful," put in Faber-Jones. "Didn't have to be, either. Very generous man."

"Well, don't let it get around, Jonesy," said Lucas Johns, making a face.

They sat down to a magnificent dinner, for although Faber-Jones had stripped himself of many of the accouterments of his past he had kept his cook and the cook's husband, who served dinner. The conversation was typical of dinner parties attended by people who had never met before: it was exploratory, impersonal, and of necessity superficial, but in this case very intelligent. Dr. Tennison talked with enthusiasm of her latest archaeological expedition. Dr. Berkowitz had recently visited the Middle East on his vacation, and he and Madame Karitska compared impressions of Afghanistan, where she had lived at one time. At the other end of the table Peter Zoehfeld talked to Lucas Johns of famines and world food shortages.

It was entirely by accident that over coffee the subject of fate arose. Madame Karitska had mentioned the Persian word *kismet* to Dr. Berkowitz, and he had nodded thoughtfully. "This is always a difficult subject philosophically," he said, "and of course the East regards fate or destiny in a very different manner from the West."

"But you," inquired Madame Karitska with interest, "do you believe in destiny?"

He hesitated and then he said quietly, "For a long period in my life I refuted everything in the way of faith or meaning. You might say I collected—even exulted in—every nihilistic book, thought, and person, and this is not difficult for we live in a very depersonalizing and negative age. But I realized one day that if I believed faith and God were mere illusions—puerile longings, you might say, for reassurance and immortality—then it was equally possible that the cult of meaninglessness and despair could also be illusory, no more nor less than the rage of adolescents who fail to understand. Have we proof of either? And disliking necrophilia I chose—as Pindar put it—to 'become what I am.'"

"And that is—?"

"A man who believes in something beyond himself even when he cannot touch it."

"What Kierkegaard calls 'the leap of faith,'" she said, smiling.

"Yes. Because, you see, as a doctor I have sometimes been in the presence of miracles. I have sat beside a patient whose recovery was scientifically impossible and he has recovered. Yes, I believe in fate. Do you, Madame Karitska?"

"Oh, definitely," she said, and briefly closing her eyes she quoted, " 'Thy lot or portion in life,' said the Caliph Ali, 'is seeking after thee; therefore be at rest from seeking after it.'"

When she opened her eyes she saw that everyone at the table was looking at them, their conversation stilled. "Do you really believe that?" asked Lucas Johns, frowning. "It certainly presupposes a rather fixed destiny, doesn't it, with no freedom of choice?"

"There is always choice, but within a certain framework," said Madame Karitska.

"Nonsense," Peter Zoehfeld said flatly. "We make our own destinies."

"Are you so sure?" Madame Karitska asked, smiling at him.

"If you accept the theory that we've lived many lives it could become possible," Lucas Johns admitted. "Sometimes I've had the feeling I've lived before. Greece did that to me when I visited it."

"For myself I agree with Mr. Zoehfeld that this is nonsense," Dr. Tennison said briskly. "As a woman I've had to fight very hard to succeed in my profession, which is, I might add, a very scientific one, as well as one difficult to make a name in. I certainly refuse to believe that I didn't have full control over it myself."

Faber-Jones said cautiously, "Maybe it's rather like being dealt a certain number of cards of varying quality, and a matter of how one plays those cards. That's called karma, isn't it? Choice, as Madame Karitska says, but within limits."

"To a rational mind this is preposterous," Zoehfeld said flatly.

"Frankly, I think we've had an overdose of rational minds in the world lately," put in Lucas Johns. "They seem to create as many problems as they solve."

"I'll tell you what," said Faber-Jones, with a mischievous glance at Madame Karitska. "We have here

among us a very gifted clairvoyant. If it's not too pre-
sumptuous—if she wouldn't feel imposed upon—"

"You?" said Lucas Johns, turning to Madame Karitska. "I don't think I like that."

She gave him a sympathetic smile. "So many people
feel uncomfortable when they learn this. As a rule,
however, I don't go about reading people's minds, so
you needn't feel uneasy. My best results come from
psychometry, the holding of an object belonging to the
person I'm reading."

"Reading?" said Zoehfeld with a skeptical laugh.
"Like a book?"

Madame Karitska shrugged.

"I find this very interesting," said Dr. Berkowitz
quietly. "Also somewhat frightening, of course."

"Fortunetelling," put in Dr. Tennison scornfully.

"I think we ought to try it, it could be very amusing,"
said Lucas Johns.

"Then let me make a suggestion," added Faber-
Jones. "Namely, that all four of you toss into a hat
some object you've worn on your person for a respectable period of time, and without any of us knowing—
and especially Madame Karitska—to whom they belong. Then you can see for yourselves whether it's
fortunetelling or art."

Dr. Tennison said impatiently, "I really don't see
any connection here between our discussion of fate, or
destiny, and this kind of crystal-gazing."

"A line can be drawn," Faber-Jones told her. "For
instance if Madame Karitska is able to predict certain
things for any of you that eventually take place, then
that would suggest, would it not, that our lives are to
some extent already laid out before us?"

"But that's impossible," said Zoehfeld.

"On the contrary," said Madame Karitska, breaking in firmly, "it is our misconception of time that makes it appear impossible. But if time doesn't exist at *all* as we know it—for instance, if future-time is exactly like past-time, except that we simply haven't caught up with it yet, haven't arrived at it yet—then it becomes not only possibility but actuality."

"Quite fascinating," murmured Dr. Berkowitz.

Dr. Tennison said reproachfully, "You, a man of science, a doctor, say that?"

"I am also a human being," he said with a faint smile.

"I'll make one more suggestion," added Faber-Jones. "To spare any—uh—unnecessary embarrassment, supposing none of you identify yourselves with the results that Madame Karitska may describe."

The four agreed to the experiment with varying degrees of enthusiasm; it was promised that there would be no cheating and that the object had to have been worn regularly over a period of some months. Mr. Faber-Jones brought a hat out of a closet and passed it around, collecting four objects in it. The hat was deposited in front of Madame Karitska on the table.

Three of the four objects were wrist watches; the fourth was a small, round, polished stone with a hole drilled in its center through which a chain might be inserted. Madame Karitska reached for this first, and examined it. So far as she could see, it had no intrinsic value at all; it was, quite simply, a stone.

There was silence, except for the scratch of a match as Mr. Zoehfeld lighted his pipe.

"This amulet or charm," she said suddenly, "has been worn in a prison."

There was a stir at this, and suspicious glances exchanged among the four; one did not expect to be seated next to a former inmate at a dinner party on Cavendish Square.

"It has been worn lately—for a number of years— by a man, but there is the strong feeling that it was worn at an earlier date by a woman. The impressions mingle but the woman's are stronger, the more deeply etched. It was she who was in prison." Madame Karitska closed her eyes, concentrating. "*Very* strong impressions," she said, trembling a little. "I feel that this woman, this woman in prison, was a very brave person, very resolute in her situation. I see barbed-wire fencing around this prison . . . a camp, really, with long low buildings and guards with—Ah," she said, nodding. "I see now, this is a concentration camp. The prisoners wear drab gray suits like pajamas, and many of them have yellow stars of David sewn on their sleeves."

One of the people present drew a sharp breath, but it was impossible to guess who it was. It was the only sound as they waited, caught by the intensity in Madame Karitska's voice.

"And there is death—and yet not death," she added in a puzzled voice, frowning. "There is despair and there is love all mingled together—all these impressions are very strong. This stone was given her by the man she loves and she worries a great deal about him. He has been ill, I think, and she worries more about him than about herself. There is the impression that he too was once in the camp but is there no longer . . . and then there is this death."

She shook her head, her eyes still closed. "The woman fingers this stone; you understand it is a very intense moment and the impressions remain here. She thinks of hope and of love, and she has great trust in this man and she—I see now, she swallows two capsules. The capsules are poison," Madame Karitska said, and opened her eyes and looked around her at the watching faces. "And yet she does not die," she added simply. "A riddle."

"Of course she would die," protested Faber-Jones.

Madame Karitska closed her eyes again, and for a long time was silent. "No," she said, "not then. I feel much horror about this. There is a coffin, people looking inside and closing the coffin, and then much later she opens her eyes and she is free." Madame Karitska smiled radiantly. "I understand now. . . . The man she loved is beside her. It is he who smuggled the poison into the camp to her. It is presumably a dead body that has been shipped out of the camp but she is alive. She opens her eyes in a dark basement room and there are people there. She is safe."

"But how?" asked Dr. Tennison.

"An antidote prepared and waiting," she said. "I can feel the risk, the suspense, the terrible, agonizing suspense of whether she will be saved in time."

"Good God," said Faber-Jones.

Madame Karitska opened her eyes and smiled. "Since then, for many years, it has been worn by that man who so miraculously saved his wife. And there is sadness," she added, "for I do not think she is alive now."

Lucas Johns opened his mouth to speak and then was silent.

"But who," said Dr. Tennison. "Which of us—"

"We pledged not to tell," Faber-Jones reminded her.

"Then how do we know that what Madame Karitska

saw is right?" protested Dr. Tennison. "A story so bizarre—"

"I will take a watch next," said Madame Karitska, interrupting her, and she placed the stone carefully to one side of her coffee cup and selected a plain gold watch set into a wide, dark-brown leather band. She held it silently for a few moments in the palm of her hand and then she put it down and with a glance at Faber-Jones said, "I wonder if I might excuse myself for a moment. There is a lavatory, I believe, adjoining the bedroom where I left my coat?"

Faber-Jones, startled, said, "Yes, but there's a much nearer one just off the hall to your right."

Madame Karitska nodded and left. She went, however, to the bedroom, which she had seen before, and was absent for nearly ten minutes. When she returned she picked up a silver watch with a black band.

"You were holding a gold watch before," pointed out Lucas Johns.

"Oh? Well, I will return to that one later," she said lightly. "Let us see what this one tells us—except I am afraid that in this case there can be no secret about whom I describe, because the impression I immediately receive is that of a very strong woman who works inside the earth, who opens tombs and collects artifacts." She was silent for a few moments before speaking again. "I will not inject any personal notes into this reading but I will say this: of major importance right now in this person's life is a project to—I see the state of South Dakota, am I right? And Indians . . . an Indian burial ground?"

"Actually," began Dr. Tennison, and then flushed.

"Yes," she admitted. "Yes, I have to say that you're right. I leave next week."

Madame Karitska said sharply, "Then I would beg of you not to, for I foresee danger for you. Not physical danger but grave psychic danger. This is a sacred burial ground."

Dr. Tennison smiled. "My dear Madame Karitska, all places that we archaeologists investigate have customarily been sacred in their time."

Madame Karitska eyed her disapprovingly. "And you do not believe that interference can bring—shall we say a response?"

"You mean," Lucas Johns said with a smile, "that spirits of the dead may be hanging about?"

Dr. Tennison laughed. "Yes, I think that's exactly what she means. Rubbish, of course."

Madame Karitska smiled gently. "Whatever I may mean or not mean, I foresee trouble. This I can tell you. You are skeptical, I see, and I am sorry but I must tell you that this experience will be bad for you. You will be—changed."

Dr. Tennison shrugged and brought out a cigarette and lighted it. "You've not convinced me, although I admit you guessed where I go next. You could, of course, have read about it in the newspapers."

"I do not read newspapers," Madame Karitska said somewhat coldly, and picked up a second watch, this one a square silver one with an alligator strap.

Holding this second watch and closing her eyes she said, "Ah, this one is most interesting. We have here a person who has lived two different lives, very distinct and separate. . . . I see the state of California, yes, and very definitely from the look of the flat roofs and the blue water I would say San Francisco. A beautiful city, is it not? There is great success there, and happiness, but for this person there comes grave trouble, very bad associates. There is—" She broke off suddenly. "I do not believe I should go on with this," she said. "I do not wish to give away this person's secret, I feel it could be dangerous."

Lucas Johns said with a grin at his host, "Some dinner party, Jonesy."

As he spoke the buzzer sounded in the hall, and they could hear Faber-Jones' valet open the door, followed by the murmur of voices. Madame Karitska said with apology, "To give an incomplete reading, this happens sometimes. You will forgive me? I will read this last watch now," she said, "and then I daresay Mr. Faber-Jones will want us to move to more comfortable chairs."

She picked up the fourth and last watch, the gold one with a dark-brown leather strap, and held it lightly in the palm of one hand. "Yes," she said, closing her eyes, and said slowly, "Yes, we have here a man of great brilliance and great—yes, great shrewdness, a man who is not what he seems to be, in fact he has been many things. He has had many names as well, I believe, and also many occupations. He was born in another country but although he has lived in this country for a long time his allegiances are still to that other country."

There was something in her voice that struck the others silent. There was an atmosphere suddenly of uneasiness.

"I feel," continued Madame Karitska, "that the name Mazda has been important in this man's life. It rests there like a shadow. This man has been a professor or teacher at one time, for I get the impression of a class-room and of students, and it was during this period that he knew this woman named Mazda. He is responsible for her death. Not only that, but I get the very strong impression that he has arranged the death of at least two other people. This has something to do with Mazda. . . . Two people, a man and a woman . . ."

"Surely this is going too far?" broke in Dr. Tennison indignantly. "First Indian burial grounds and now a murderer among us?"

"This man is now working in—I see the city of New York, and one particular building in New York. . . . I believe," said Madame Karitska, opening her eyes and looking directly at Peter Zoehfeld, "it's the United Nations building."

"I *beg* your pardon!" snapped Zoehfeld, and looking highly incensed he rose from his chair. "Look here, I didn't come to your dinner party to be insulted," he told Faber-Jones. "I daresay you didn't expect it either but I don't intend to listen to any more of this claptrap. No, no, I'll accept no apology. If you'll ask your man to bring me my coat I'll leave."

"I don't wonder," sniffed Dr. Tennison.

Faber-Jones, looking puzzled, said, "I really don't understand—I mean, actually, you know . . . I mean, I'm dreadfully sorry." He gave Madame Karitska a quick, helpless glance. "I feel responsible, of course—a parlor game, you know, I didn't dream—"

Tight-lipped, Zoehfeld said, "Never mind, I'll just *go*."

He turned on his heel and stalked out of the room.

Dr. Tennison turned and gave Madame Karitska an indignant stare. "You do a great deal of harm with your crystal-ball reading, my dear woman. I hope you realize that."

But Madame Karitska chose instead to answer Faber-Jones' questioning gaze. "There are policemen outside in your hall waiting for him," she said quietly. "When I asked about your lavatory I actually wanted to use the telephone in the bedroom. I called Lieutenant Pruden at the hospital and he understood at once what to do."

"Good God," said Lucas Johns, "you mean the man actually is a murderer?"

Looking appalled, Faber-Jones said, "But how would Pruden know what to do? How could you be that sure?"

She smiled. "Because some weeks ago Lieutenant Pruden brought to me the watch of a man named Dr. Bugov who disappeared three years ago here in Trafton. The impressions I received when I picked up Mr. Zoehfeld's watch were identical to the impressions I received from Dr. Bugov's watch. They are the same man."

"I think," said Dr. Tennison with a shudder, "that I too choose to leave now, but not because I am a murderess, I just think we've all had enough, don't you? I'm very tired."

"Yes," said Dr. Berkowitz with a start, "I think you're quite right."

"No offense meant, Jonesy," said Lucas Johns, "but I think I'll go too. Really the most dramatic dinner party I've attended in years."

They arose and exchanged the usual murmurs of thank-yous as Faber-Jones' valet brought out hats, scarfs, and coats. Dr. Tennison was the first to leave, kissing Faber-Jones good-by and shaking Madame Karitska's hand. Lucas Johns left next, with a long look into Madame Karitska's eyes and an inexplicable "Thank you."

"And you I'll see again on Tuesday," Faber-Jones told Dr. Berkowitz, shaking his hand. Seeing the doctor look blank he added, "My annual check-up day, you know."

"Oh—oh yes," said Dr. Berkowitz, and put on his coat, which was nearly as wrinkled as his suit. He looked extraordinarily tired.

"I think you are forgetting something, Dr. Berkowitz," Madame Karitska told him as he moved toward the door.

He turned and looked at her blankly, his thoughts obviously elsewhere.

"Your wife's amulet," she said, holding it out to him in the palm of her hand. "The stone she wore in Buchenwald."

He stared at the object in her hand and then he lifted his eyes to hers and nodded. "Thank you," he said quietly. "You—brought it all back, you know. She was very dear to me, and still is. Thank you."

When the door had closed behind him Faber-Jones said incredulously, *"Dr. Berkowitz?* I thought surely Lucas Johns—"

She shook her head. "Lucas Johns was in the recording business in San Francisco and ran into great trouble. When he gave evidence against the criminals who'd broken his life the authorities gave him a new name and new identity. No, not Lucas Johns. His was the reading I shortened, to spare his feelings."

"But kind, mousy, little Dr. Berkowitz?"

Madame Karitska reached out and affectionately touched his cheek with her hand. "Oh my dear Mr. Faber-Jones," she said, "do you really think heroes are six feet tall and swash-buckling? That man is probably the most heroic man you will ever meet."

"And he'll give me a check-up on Tuesday and talk about the weather and gall bladders," groaned Faber-Jones.

Chapter 12

"It's really distressed me a great deal," Faber-Jones said, sitting on Madame Karitska's couch and staring into his cup of coffee. "The man seemed absolutely charming during those two hours we spent trapped in the subway, and now——"

"He *was* charming," pointed out Madame Karitska. "Always. But charm is artificially acquired, it has nothing to do with essence."

"I feel——I know it's irrational but I feel somewhat responsible for his death."

Madame Karitska regarded him with impatience. "My dear Faber-Jones, how could you possibly know that Peter Zoehfeld was going to swallow a capsule of cyanide at the first opportunity after his arrest? Four days ago you felt dazed but really quite triumphant that a foreign agent had been uncloaked at your dinner party. Today—"

"Today Zoehfeld's dead, which makes a difference."

"On the contrary, my dear friend, death was by his own choice. What was not choice for either of you, I think, was meeting on a subway train in New York City."

"You really think that? You really believe these things are—*arranged?*" His voice was skeptical.

"The large events, yes. We earn them, we attract them by what we are and what we have been. For the large events of our lives I believe we're moved about like pieces on a chessboard. We assume with the utmost vanity that our thoughts and our plans for the future are entirely our own, but the mind is vacant until thoughts are placed there, is it not, and can any of us trace our thoughts to their source? A person will assume it is he alone who suddenly decides to accept a job a thousand miles away in a strange city, thereby meeting the one person important for him to know— for good or evil—at that point in his life and in his development. Or two strangers meet on a subway train, and one is brought back to Trafton where three years ago he killed two people." She shrugged. "I believe Jung called these juxtapositions of fate 'meaningful coincidences.' They deeply interested him, as they should everyone. But we live in a whole network—a universe—of meaningful coincidences."

"I don't see exactly how that would apply—"

"One can sometimes see this when one looks back, through hindsight."

"You mean taking a major event in one's life, I suppose, and examining all the threads that went into producing it. But that implies that the people we meet—"

"Must be treated with infinite respect," she said firmly, "for few of them arrive casually in our lives. Some, yes, but others—" She broke off at the sound of a knock at her door.

Faber-Jones put down his cup and reached for his attaché case. "You have an appointment?"

"No, but people still arrive without them." She rose and walked to the door with him. "I'm glad you stopped in," she said, opening the door, and then in surprise, "Lieutenant Pruden!"

"Well, well," cried Faber-Jones, wringing his hand. "Your first day back at work, isn't it? I must say you're looking fit."

Pruden grinned at Madame Karitska. "Yes, and the first assignment I've been handed is to investigate a witch so I'm here for a little expertise."

"A witch!" said Madame Karitska, laughing.

"Not really—I don't *think*—but she may end up getting burned at the stake if I don't find the answer to what's happening."

"Then I'll leave you both to your consultation on witches," said Faber-Jones. "By the way, John Painter's cutting his third record this afternoon," he called over his shoulder to Madame Karitska.

When he had gone she said, "Tell me about your witch."

"Do you have any appointments for the next hour?"

Madame Karitska shook her head.

"Then I'm hoping you'll come with me. You see, I can't even get in, there are four dogs roaming the yard and—"

"Four dogs! You wish me to protect you from four dogs, to—how do you say it?—run interference for you?"

"Now you're laughing at me," Pruden told her accusingly. "I'm a convalescent hero and you're laughing at me. Actually I thought if she saw a woman with me at the gate—I'm sure I saw her face at the window; she must have seen me tangling with the dogs, which she could easily have called off if she had felt like it. She's a recluse, you see. I might have asked for a policewoman but could a policewoman tell me, once I get inside—if I can—whether the woman's a witch or not?"

"You believe, then, in witches," Madame Karitska said, her eyes dancing at him humorously.

"I keep reading about them in the newspapers. Covens and all that. Are there such things?"

"No comment," she said, and picked up her purse. "Shall we go?"

"Good. It's not far away, it's on Mulberry Street, off First Avenue near the river. I hope it won't take long," he added as he helped her into his car outside.

"Tell me why the police have been called in," she suggested.

He climbed in beside her and they drove off. "Nothing's too clear to me yet. It seems that some very odd things have been happening in the neighborhood lately. First a young boy became ill—turned wild, someone said—and then a sixteen-year-old girl came close to having convulsions on the street and rumor started that they were each under a spell. The cop on the beat picked up some of the gossip over a period of several weeks, so I began by interviewing him this morning. But the police were officially called in last night when a third person—another sixteen-year-old girl—went beserk, found her father's pistol, and began taking pot shots at windows. She had to be placed in a strait jacket. The weird thing is that she's quite normal this morning, they tell me, and remembers nothing about it except feeling terrible."

"LSD?" suggested Madame Karitska.

"Possibly, but the man sent over last night said the girl has no history of drug-taking—none of them do—and this morning she violently denied taking any drugs."

"And the witch?"

He sighed. "I'm not sure we've made much progress in the last two hundred years. Nobody knows who this woman is, but she lives on the street and a few of the neighbors have decided that she's responsible for it, and that she's bewitching the children. If it weren't for those dogs of hers," he said grimly, "they'd probably have stormed the house last night and lynched her. I hope not, but some investigations are overdue."

"Obviously," said Madame Karitska.

They turned off Broad Street into an area near the river. It was a neighborhood that had once been elegant until, around the turn of the century, it had slipped into the worst kind of slum, and then during Trafton's renaissance era ten years ago the neighborhood had become the target of a renewal project and was now a street of middle-class homes, all of them brownstones, some detached and some attached. They were set back from the street with small grassy plots in front of them and handsome, old-fashioned wrought-iron fences. There were only two buildings on the street that did not match the well-groomed exteriors: one was an auto-body shop in the middle of the block, a rambling frame building badly in need of paint and surrounded by weeds and skeletons of cars rusting in the yard; the other was a boarded-over brownstone almost suffocated by trees and shrubbery that grew up all around it and isolated it from the others. It was at this seemingly abandoned house that Pruden stopped.

"According to the city tax office—I've had a busy morning—her name is Mrs. Eva Trumbull."

"But there's no glass in any of the windows, only boards," protested Madame Karitska. "Are you sure there's someone living inside?"

"People see her come out at night. Apparently to ride on her broomstick," he said grimly.

As they climbed out of the car a small boy rode up on his tricycle and stared at them. "You're not going in *there,* are you?" he demanded incredulously. "She'll give you the evil eye, she'll turn you into a gingerbread boy."

"Ah—'Hansel and Gretel,' " said Madame Karitska, nodding.

"No—brainwashing," said Pruden.

"Unless, of course, she *is* a witch," offered Madame Karitska innocently. She was looking over the gate into a jungle of green, with only a narrow tunnel leading to the house. "How do you propose we advance, singly, with me first?"

"Of course not," said Pruden, but he was too late; Madame Karitska had already dislodged the rope that tied the gate closed and had entered the leafy green tunnel. At once the sound of barking could be heard, and four large dogs raced down the tunnel toward them.

"Good morning," said Madame Karitska in a calm voice, standing very still and beginning a small conversation with them.

Pruden, just behind her, fought back an instinct to retreat. He stood bemused as the dogs slowed, regarded Madame Karitska with suspicion, and then stopped, staring at her with curiosity. They were wild mangy-looking creatures, the last sort of dog Pruden would have cared to confront, but they stood with cocked heads, as if listening. Madame Karitska spoke to them very simply, explaining that she had no wish to trespass, they they were fine watchdogs but that she had business with their mistress and would like to visit her. Pruden, listening, thought that her voice exuded a powerfully tranquilizing sense of love. It was uncanny; he could feel his own tensions relaxing and melting away.

"And now," said Madame Karitska, slowly stretching out one hand to them, "we are going to walk toward the house. You will allow this?"

One of the dogs growled, then walked to the extended hand and sniffed it. "Yes," murmured Madame Karitska, not moving. "As you see, I am no threat at all to your mistress. You feel this? It is so."

And with this, her voice growing firm and commanding, she took a step forward. Meeting with no resistance she said to Pruden, "I think we can walk to the steps now. Remain calm and move slowly."

And so they moved toward the steps, three of the dogs accompanying them with the gravity of sentinels, the fourth frolicking along behind, with a lamentable tendency to sniff at Pruden's heels. As Madame Karitska set foot on the porch Pruden heard the sound of numerous locks being disengaged. The door opened. A gruff voice said, "What did you do to them? Who are you?"

"I made them my friends," said Madame Karitska, "and we've come to tell you that your neighbors think you're a witch and you may be in some danger from this."

The door opened wider. "Come in," the disembodied voice said, and they entered.

What they entered was another tunnel not unlike the garden tunnel they had just left, except that here their passage lay between stacks of magazines and newspapers piled to the ceiling. In the dim murk of this hallway stood a small, thin woman wearing what looked to Pruden like an assortment of burlap bags tied around her waist and covered by a long black coat festooned with one large safety pin. Her feet were in old white sneakers. Her hair was gray and piled high on her head; her face, indistinct in the gloom, nevertheless looked human and intelligent. Looking them over keenly she turned on her heel and said, "In here." Pruden saw that she limped badly, one foot dragging behind her.

She led them through tunnels of cartons and old furniture into a large room full of other maze-like tunnels until they came at last to a small cleared area facing a window that looked out upon what must have once been a rear garden. It was the only window not covered over by boards, and gave Pruden a glimpse of what this house must once have been. In this area, perhaps nine by six, stood a battered couch on which several blankets were heaped. In front of the couch stood a card table holding an electric hot plate, several plates, a tin mug, a knife, fork, and spoon, and un-opened cans of food. Pruden realized that this was where Eva Trumbull lived, ate, and slept. The Department of Health, he thought, would certainly not approve of this.

"If I'd known I was going to have guests," the woman said with dignity, "I'd have put on my dress. I have a very good dress," she explained to Madame Karitska and for just a second her eyes flashed.

In the light from the window Pruden saw that she was younger than he'd thought at first, and proud. Very proud, he thought, noticing the way she held her head, the way she ignored any impressions the room might have on them, refusing to explain or to apologize but looking at them fiercely and squarely, almost defiantly. She was tough as a nut, and proud. It was probably the reality of her helplessness that had made her tough; the helpless didn't survive for long.

"A witch indeed," she was saying to Madame Karit-ska with a sniff. "I'm not a witch, and I'm not a pauper either, no matter what you may be thinking."

She ignored Pruden, speaking to Madame Karitska alone, and Pruden admitted he couldn't have handled the interrogation half as well. She said that she owned the house free and clear and that it had been her home long before the accident. It had been a car accident, she said, and her husband and only child had been killed and she'd been left crippled. She didn't want charity, and she couldn't help it if the neighbors thought her unfriendly, but nobody had ever come to see her, and she couldn't get around or out much. "Except at night," she said.

"And what do you do at night?" asked Madame Karitska.

"Collect junk," she said. "I take my son's wagon and bring home junk. I sell it, it's my income."

"This isn't a very safe way for you to live," said Pruden. "All these newspapers and magazines—"

"Well, I'm not much of a housekeeper," she said bluntly. "Doesn't seem any reason to be, if you know what I mean. And two of the dogs sleep inside every night—"

Pruden had already guessed this from the smell.

"—and two stand guard outside. They take turns. Very intelligent dogs," she added, and her face lighted up at this.

Madame Karitska nodded and rose. "Thank you for talking to us, I think we'll be going now but we'll be back. I will at least," she said with a quick glance at Pruden. "We appreciate your letting us in."

"My dogs liked you," the woman said, her face softening. "The children on the block—oh, I hear what they say sometimes. If it weren't for my dogs—"

She left the rest unspoken, escorted them back through the tunnels of junk to the door, and opened it for them.

Once outside Madame Karitska said, "I hope you're not going to report this."

"I really should," he told her in a troubled voice.

"It isn't as if she were eighty years old. She seems quite healthy."

"What did you think of her?"

"Very lonely," said Madame Karitska briskly, "but not at all sorry for herself. She has, I think, made her peace with life. She's narrowed it down to what she can manage and closed out the rest. In her way she is probably happier than anyone on this street."

"How can you say that?" asked Pruden, startled.

"Because she's stripped her life to the essentials," pointed out Madame Karitska. "Quite Tao, actually. There is a line in one of the translations of *The Way* that goes—" She stopped at the gate, closing her eyes for a moment. " 'In the pursuit of learning, every day something is acquired. In the pursuit of Tao, every day something is dropped.' "

"You think her a middle-aged hippie then?" said Pruden, amused.

She regarded him with exasperation. "When I was young, my dear Lieutenant, the eccentrics were what gave life flavor and excitement. They no longer seem to be tolerated in America now, which seems a great pity. Your Thoreau was an eccentric, and your Emerson was no conformist. Can you wonder that your young people court eccentricity and individuality when so many adults are predictable and bland? She is eccentric but she is *not* a witch."

"I didn't think so," Pruden said, opening the door of his car. "I'll take you home. I've got to interview the girl who shot out windows last night."

"Is there," asked Madame Karitska, "any reason I cannot accompany you?"

"Well, it's not exactly regulations but I certainly don't want to be accused of being predictable and bland," he said grinning. "It's only across the street, let's go."

The steps of number 813 were occupied by a very pretty young girl of fifteen or sixteen, and two boys somewhat older. Madame Karitska looked them over casually, one by one: her impression of the girl was one of long tanned legs, long blond hair, and a sense of self-importance. The boy on her right closely resembled her, his hair very blond, his face healthily flushed with sun tan, but he looked hostile, his eyes like splinters of glass. The boy on the left was dark and intense, his eyes admiring as they rested on the girl.

Pruden introduced himself and displayed his ID card. "I'm looking for a Miss Kathy Dunlap."

"That's me," the girl said eagerly. "Is it about last night?"

Pruden nodded.

"Well, I'm Kathy and this is my brother Birch," she said, pointing to the blond boy beside her. "I guess you'd like to go inside, right? My mother doesn't like me to talk to strangers." She stood up and brushed off her skirt.

"And who are you?" Madame Karitska asked the unintroduced young man.

Kathy said carelessly, "Oh, that's Joe Lister, he works at the auto-body shop. So long, Joe."

Lister turned scarlet and stood up. Putting his hands in his pockets he mumbled, "See ya," and slouched off, looking considerably diminished by Kathy's indifference.

Mrs. Dunlap was summoned from upstairs and came into the living room looking harassed. "It was terrible, just terrible," she said. "It went on nearly the whole night and we couldn't get a doctor; it was Sunday you know, their day off, and the hospital told us to bring Kathy in but we simply couldn't get her into the car. Please sit down, won't you?"

The chairs were arranged very symmetrically and as Pruden sat down, inadvertently moving one, he saw the pained look on Mrs. Dunlap's face. He carefully moved the chair back in line with the other. "Can you explain how she acted?"

"Delirious," said Mrs. Dunlap simply. "Out of her head completely and yet no fever, no fever at all. She wouldn't sit down, she wouldn't lie down, she roamed the whole house—babbling—and when we tried to get her to rest she screamed at us. It was terrible."

"What do you remember of it?" Pruden asked Kathy.

"That's what everyone's asking," she said, "but—well, it was like waking up from a nightmare this morning. I can't remember anything except how horrid the nightmare was. I was exhausted. Mum made me stay in bed until ten. I still feel restless and itchy," she admitted, "but I don't remember any gun at all, or screaming, or anything like that."

"It's my husband's gun, all properly registered," the woman added hurriedly. "He has a very nice collection of guns in the basement. He's a member of the Target Club. And we did *not* call the woman across the street a witch, as people are saying."

"Did you happen to notice if the pupils of Kathy's eyes were dilated?"

Mrs. Dunlap indignantly shook her head. "No, I didn't notice. But I can assure you, Lieutenant, that both my children are *good* children. Birch," she said with a proud glance at her son, "is a top honor student at school, he studies hard and gets all A's. Kathy isn't quite an honor student but she's on the Dean's List. We're very strict with them, I can assure you, and if either of them so much as touched drugs they know their father'd whip them. We find this terribly embarrassing, all of it."

Pruden hazarded the guess that Kathy didn't find it embarrassing but was rather enjoying the attention. "Yes— well . . ." he murmured, and stood up.

"I'll see you to the door, sir," Birch said, jumping to his feet.

"Well, at least the boy had manners," Pruden said when they were on the street again. "Any impressions?"

"Only as we approached them on the street," said Madame Karitska. "I felt a sharp stab of alarm, of something being very wrong, but of course something *has* been very wrong, or was last night."

Pruden stopped and looked up at the second floor, where a glazier was fitting glass into one of the windows. "Some of these model children don't always tell their parents about their less model-like experiments, of course. I just wish a doctor had been called." He consulted his memo book. "Crystal Jamison's away for three days—her grandmother died—so we can't call on her. Let's see if Johnny Larkin's family called a doctor."

"The first child to become ill?"

He nodded and guided her to his car. "Around the block, next street."

The Larkin family turned out to be very different from the Dunlaps. Nothing was symmetrical in their living room, which was filled with plants, a coffee table piled high with books, and a weaver's loom crowded into one corner. Mrs. Larkin wore dungarees and a sweat shirt and apparently had a sense of humor. "I'll call him," she said, "if I can pry him away from his microscope. Meals don't do it, maybe a live policeman will."

Johnny, when he arrived, turned out to be a very small twelve-year-old with auburn hair, glasses, and the gravity of an adult. His mother very tactfully withdrew, leaving him alone with Pruden and Madame Karitska.

He nodded to Pruden's query about a doctor. "Yes, he came, Mother called him, which I really didn't think awfully necessary. I certainly wasn't as sick as I hear Kathy was."

"And what did the doctor say?"

"He said I had to have been taking drugs," Johnny said firmly. "Except I hadn't taken any. Of course," he added scrutinizing Pruden frankly, "you needn't believe that. The doctor didn't."

"How did you feel?" asked Pruden. "Can you remember?"

"Oh yes," Johnny said, to his surprise. "I like to observe things and I wasn't that sick. The pupils of my eyes were dilated—huge, actually—and I couldn't see very well. I minded that most of all, you know—I couldn't read or look through my microscope, which made it awfully dull. At first I felt very lightheaded but then I became what I think you'd call 'manic.' I had a terrifying amount of energy. I finally went out in the yard and built a stone wall. You can see it if you'd like," he said generously. "I had the feeling, you know, that if I didn't use this terrible energy I'd go quite mad. My father says I carried rocks that he couldn't have carried, and he weighs two hundred."

"And you?" asked Madame Karitska with a smile.

"Ninety-eight pounds."

Pruden said with respect, "Have you any—uh—theories about this, Johnny? For one thing it does seem to be only young people who've been experiencing this—this—"

"Phenomenon?" suggested Johnny. "But that's not true, you know. Cas Johnson said he'd had it too, and he's twenty-four, I think."

"Cas Johnson," echoed Pruden.

Johnny nodded. "He works part time at the auto-body shop."

"That would be Lister's auto-body shop?"

Johnny stood up and walked to a rear window. "As you can see, it's directly in back of our house, it's how I cut through to school and to my friends on Mulberry Street. It's got a great yard for playing catch and everything and Mr. Lister never minds our hanging out there. He's a really relaxed guy. And then we used to sit in the old junked cars when we were kids and pretend we were driving." He explained this as if it were a century ago. "They brought Daredevil Demon's car there last week," he added in an awed voice. "It was right there in Mr. Lister's auto-body shop for six days. We were in school when Daredevil Demon came for it though." This made him sad; he looked sad, as if being twelve was a cross to be born.

"Well, Johnny, you've been very helpful," Pruden said, rising. "If you remember anything else I'd certainly appreciate your letting me know."

"I'd be glad to," the boy said gravely. "I can go back to my work now?"

Pruden nodded, and he left.

"And what did *you* think of the doctor's diagnosis?"

Pruden asked Mrs. Larkin when she met them in the hall.

Johnny's mother considered this thoughtfully. "I thought it a little ridiculous, actually. Of course I refuse to be the kind of mother who insists her son can do no wrong and won't try something *once*. As you can see from meeting Johnny, he *could* try something once, being, alas, hopelessly scientific even about how he eats his breakfast. But I also believe him when he says he took nothing druggy because he knows he can tell us the truth, and he never lies. He has," she added reflectively, "a scientific respect for truth."

"The scientific part I certainly noticed," Pruden said dryly.

Mrs. Larkin laughed. "I thought you might. By the way, is Mrs. Trumbull a bona fide witch? I do horoscopes myself, and I'm tremendously interested in that sort of thing."

"No, she's not a witch. You've met her?"

Mrs. Larkin shook her head. "No, I've never stopped in. The dogs, you know . . ." She looked a trifle guilty.

They left, and with a glance at her watch Madame Karitska announced that she would have to get back to her apartment now. "Reluctantly," she added, "but I have a half-past-one-o'clock appointment. You are very good, you know; this has been very instructive, observing you at work."

"Thanks," said Pruden, feeling inordinately pleased. "Climb in, I'll drop you off."

That was Monday. On Wednesday Pruden phoned and said flatly, "I thought you'd want to know—"

"Mrs. Trumbull?" said Madame Karitska.

Pruden was somewhat taken aback. "What makes you say that?"

"Because I had an impression of change hanging over her, something for the better. I felt confident for her."

"Well, your ESP must have suffered a short circuit," he said grimly, "because one of her dogs got out of the yard yesterday and attacked a child. A neighbor beat off the dog with a stick and called the police. The child was taken to the hospital—twenty wounds needed cauterizing—and has had to begin rabies injections."

"Plakhoy," murmured Madame Karitska, lapsing into the language of her childhood. "But this is bad, very bad," she explained.

"Exactly," he went on. "The police notified the ASPCA and Mrs. Trumbull was ordered to bring her dogs to the shelter today, but she didn't show up. Now she's been given a summons to appear tomorrow in Magistrate's Court."

"The poor woman. But," added Madame Karitska thoughtfully, "she does have a dress. She said so."

"Very funny," growled Pruden. "What I particularly called about, though, is that I've gone to see her and she's very upset at leaving her house unattended in the daytime. She liked you. When I asked her what could be done for her she wondered if you could possibly house-sit. Unfortunately," he added, "we can't spare a policeman for that sort of thing."

"Obviously," said Madame Karitska.

"Feeling is running high about her, I might add, although I think you'd be safe enough. Not entirely because of the dog," he added. "Somebody else has become ill."

"Who?"

"A seventeen-year-old girl—same neighborhood—named Julie Austen. She's been taken to the hospital, so maybe this time our mysterious ailment can be identified."

"I'm sorry to hear that. At what time should I present myself at Mrs. Trumbull's house tomorrow?"

"You'll do it? Great. I'd suggest half past twelve. She's due in court at one o'clock. She shouldn't be there more than an hour or two at most."

"Tell her I'll be there at twelve twenty-five," said Madame Karitska, and hanging up the telephone she picked it up again to begin rearranging two of her afternoon appointments for the next day.

At half past twelve the next day Mrs. Trumbull left for Magistrate's Court looking very neat in a dark-blue dress and a curious sort of hat that Madame Karitska yearned to bring into the twentieth century with a few adjustments. Since Mrs. Trumbull had no money for taxi fare, Pruden had offered to take her to court in his car; she wrung Madame Karitska's hand, asked her to explain matters to her three remaining dogs, and climbed in beside Pruden, looking very small, anxious and defenseless.

Madame Karitska closed the gate behind her, chatted with the dogs for a few minutes, and then went into the house. Its darkness was oppressive and she headed for Mrs. Trumbull's microscopic living area where at least the darkness had been lightened into mere gloom. She sat for a long time on the couch, opening herself up to the feel of the house, and then she began to walk up and down the aisles of towering cartons and piles of newspapers, feeling drawn to them as if somewhere in the maze lay something of importance to Mrs. Trumbull's future. But only a few of the cartons lay open, and she had no flashlight; what she did find, however, was an ancient pair of grass clippers. Carrying these she went outside, looked over the jungle of green, and glanced at her watch. An hour had already passed; she decided that she might as well make herself useful, and with some humor began to attack the path to the house.

She was hard at work when the gate opened and Johnny Larkin's mother walked in. Once the dogs had been quieted she said rather breathlessly, "I hope you don't mind. Lieutenant Pruden stopped at the house this morning—he wanted Johnny to remember and write down everywhere he'd been the day he became sick— and he said you'd be here while Mrs. Trumbull's at court. I think it's perfectly splendid of you. I've brought you some lunch."

"It's very kind of you," said Madame Karitska, "but I had lunch before I came."

Mrs. Larkin nodded. "Then I'll save it for Mrs. Trumbull. I made her a cake, chocolate with three layers." Looking around her she said, "It really is a mess, isn't it? I suppose she just didn't have the energy to keep *up*. The housewives' nightmare," she added with a grin. "You catch the flu and lose a week and it's overwhelming how behind you can get." Sobering, she said, "You know, if people didn't insist she was a witch —this really is a nice neighborhood—we could all pitch in and do something about this."

Madame Karitska said gently, with a faint smile, "Yes indeed. It would be so helpful, wouldn't it?"

The gate creaked again, the dogs came running, and

Madame Karitska turned to see a man and a young woman standing in the tunnel of green and looking somewhat appalled. She quieted the dogs and looked at them questioningly.

"Inspector Fowler from the Department of Housing," the man said gruffly. "And Miss Wyler from the Department of Welfare. We've come to inspect the house and remove the dogs for examination. Magistrate's Court sent us."

"But Mrs. Trumbull?" asked Madame Karitska, brows lifting.

"She's still at court. She'll be there until our investigation's finished and the magistrate makes a recommendation. A few more hours."

"So we'll just go in," the young woman said with a smile.

It did not take long for the house to be declared uninhabitable. Every room in the building was piled high with junk, with only narrow aisles for access. There was a thirty-foot well in the basement, and around this were arranged a number of perishable food items and two buckets. There was no electricity, no running water, and no toilet facilities. "I've never seen anything like it," the building inspector said incredulously. "One match and the whole place could blow up."

"And she insists she needs no help from welfare," said Miss Wyler sadly, looking around her. "Well, we'd better go back and report."

When they had gone Mrs. Larkin looked at Madame Karitska. "You're going to have a long wait."

"Yes," said Madame Karitska.

"I'll just go home and put a casserole in the oven

and then I'll come back and wait with you. I feel," she added vaguely, "somehow responsible. You know, 'no man is an island,' and all that."

It was six o'clock before Pruden walked in the gate; he came alone. "Still here?" he said.

"Still here," Madame Karitska told him with a smile. "But where is Mrs. Trumbull?"

"I'll take you both home," he said in a hard voice. "They've sent Mrs. Trumbull to Harlow Hospital for two days of testing to see whether she's sane, and Julie Austen died half an hour ago in the hospital."

"Died!" cried Mrs. Larkin. "Oh no, *Julie?* Only seventeen and *dead?*"

"Yes," Pruden said grimly. "The nearest they can get to it is belladonna poisoning but they're not sure." With a glance at the house he added, "They're posting a guard here. I explained the circumstances and they don't want trouble so they'll post a guard. Let's go," he said in a savage voice, and turned on his heel and led them to his car.

"Belladonna," Pruden said the following day when he stopped in, exhausted, at Madame Karitska's. "Also called deadly nightshade, devil's cherries, devil's herb, and great morel. I don't get it, frankly. Seven patrolmen spent the entire morning combing the back yards of the neighborhood, especially Joe's auto-body shop where the weeds are thickest, and none of them found any deadly nightshade. And even if they did, why would four people go out and eat the stuff?"

"What is interesting to me," said Madame Karitska, "is the pattern of the illnesses."

"What do you mean?"

"Johnny Larkin was only mildly ill. You tell me that Cas Johnson was a trifle sicker—it was necessary for him to report out of work for two days. Kathy Dunlap went berserk and Julie Austen died."

Pruden's brows lifted. "I'm not following you."

She said calmly, lighting a cigarette in a long jade holder, "To me it gives the impression of someone— shall we say fumbling for the right dosage?"

He stared at her incredulously. "You're implying *murder?*"

She looked at him steadily. "This hadn't occurred to you?"

Startled, he said, "Actually, no, but then no one died until last night. And when you discover it's a weed that grows wild—"

"You would have come to the possibility eventually," she assured him, "but perhaps not until someone else had died. Did Johnny Larkin give you a—a *scientific* listing of the places he'd visited before he became ill?"

He nodded. "It's here somewhere." He groped in his pocket and brought out several lists. "Cas Johnson did it for me, too, and Kathy Dunlap. But look here, why do you suspect a human hand in this?"

"Let me look at them a moment," said Madame Karitska, interrupting him, and studied the three lists with interest.

"I know what you'll find," Pruden said with a rueful smile. "There's just one common denominator, one place they all visited before becoming sick."

"Yes, the auto-body shop," said Madame Karitska, nodding, and glanced at her watch. "I feel it's important we go there. Will you take me right now?"

The senior Joe Lister was a large, slow-moving man with a round, cheerful face. He turned off the sanding machine with which he'd been removing paint from a crumpled fender and wiped his fingers carefully on his jeans before shaking hands. His garage held two cars as well as the truck on which he was working, each in various stages of deshabille; there were more cars waiting outside. "Hey, Cas," he shouted, "take over, will you?" His helper started up the sanding machine again and Lister beckoned them toward the rear.

"Rush job," he apologized. "We can talk better in here." Behind a window set into the wall lay an untidy office with a desk. He opened the door and led them inside.

"Yeah, the kids hang out here a lot," he said in reply to Pruden's questions. "It don't bug me at all. Hell, kids like grease and dirt. Every once in a while somebody starts up a petition to get the shop off the street—usually somebody just moved here—but hell, a few weeks later they forget about it, they're glad to know where their kids are. There's a Coke machine out in the corner near the door to the yard, and there's usually a pot of coffee going. . . . I don't mind, I like kids. Got two myself."

"We met your son Joe," said Madame Karitska pleasantly. "At the Dunlap house."

"At the house but I'll bet not in it," he said with a short laugh. "And that *does* bug me, Joe being as good as anybody on this street, and my shop being a place they all practically grew up in, but the girls on this block—Kathy in particular—look down their noses at him. Yeah, that bugs me," he said. "I don't like that."

"Does Joe mind?" asked Pruden.

"Mind? Of course he minds. He's nuts about that Dunlap girl and she plays him like a fish on a line. But what're you going to do?" he asked with a shrug. "They have to learn the hard way."

Pruden nodded, his gaze moving around the office. "I wonder if you could tell me what chemicals you use here, or have stored in the building. Anything exotic? Anything you may have had for years and forgotten about?"

It was stuffy in the office. Seeing Pruden take out his notebook, presumably to make lists, Madame Karitska excused herself, saying, "I'll be outside, Lieutenant."

He nodded absently and she went out, closing the door behind her. Cas Johnson was leaning over the crumpled fender, the sanding machine still buzzing like an angry insect. Beyond him, on the street, she saw Mrs. Larkin talking animatedly to an elderly man with a cane. Madame Karitska turned to the right, toward the small door that led into the yard with its tall grass and rusting cars. Next to the door, just inside it, she saw the Coke machine that Lister had mentioned, and beside it, on a shelf, a hot plate, a water kettle already near the boiling point, several jars of instant coffee, and a bag of sugar. Still more interesting, she thought, was the bulletin board hanging over the coffee shelf. This more than any of Lister's words spelled out the part which the auto-body shop played in the neighborhood. It was festooned with handwritten signs: *KATHY, report home before your music lessons. Important, Mother. For Sale—one piano, see Larkins after 7 P.M.* A family named Maraziti had three kittens free to anyone who could give them a good home. Birch Dunlap had a ukelele for sale, and Butch Jamison was ready to trade his Batman cards for some aggies.

Madame Karitska wondered what aggies were.

She walked out into the sun, vaguely inspected some of the cars waiting for repair, and then felt drawn to a shady corner with a bench at the side of the garage. She sat down and studied the sunny yard around her, her glance eventually falling on a thick growth of horizontal stalks which she recognized as a plant that grew thickly in Russia. Southern Russia, she remembered. Its name was . . . was . . .

She was lost in thought when Pruden found her. "I thought you wanted to interview Joe Lister senior," he said accusingly. "You stayed only about three minutes."

"Yes," she said.

"I'm beginning to wonder about Joe junior. Lister says——"

"I heard," she said, lifting one arm to point. "Over there."

"Over there what? You look strange."

"I think," she said, "that I am staring at your poisonous plant."

"Here? Belladonna?"

"Not belladonna. I've been trying to remember its generic name; it grows all along the coast of the Black Sea in Russia. Datura Stramonium, that's it. In Europe it's called thorn apple." She rose and walked over to the horizontal stems. "It's September and it's in seed now," she pointed out. "These look like berries but they're seeds." She plucked a stalk and brought it to him. "They're fully as poisonous as belladonna. They produce giddiness, dilation of the pupils of the eyes. . . ."

Pruden stared at the plant, thinking that he'd never seen anything so modest look so evil. Nature supplied most of her seeds with lavish colors—green, red, white, yellow—but these were dark brown, nearly black, a dozen of them to each stem, like tiny beads. There were no leaves, only the thin upright stalk and the slender sheath bearing this lacy frond of brownish-black seeds. He said abruptly, "I'll call our lab man."

He turned—they both turned—at a sudden cry from the door. Mrs. Larkin stood there with her mouth open, a cup dangling from one finger. Her eyes looked huge and frightened, her lips framed words that the sanding machine behind her blotted out. With a look of astonishment she slumped forward and fell to the ground.

Pruden rushed to her side and stretched her flat on the grass, pried open the lid of one eye and nodded. "Dilated." He stood up and shouted "Lister!" and then rushed inside to silence the sanding machine.

Madame Karitska was already hurrying along the path and through a gap in the board fence to the Larkin house. She walked into the kitchen, found the spices in a cabinet over the sink, and returned to the garage; it was the first time Pruden had seen her run.

"Every minute counts," she told him. "Tepid water and a tablespoonful of this powdered mustard. She'll need a stomach pump, you've called an ambulance?"

Pruden nodded. Lister was already bringing a glass of water. "Barely warm," he said.

"Spoon," said Madame Karitska.

Cas Johnson brought a spoon. They propped up Mrs. Larkin while Madame Karitska stirred the mustard into the water. Mrs. Larkin, opening her eyes, said very clearly and indignantly, "That green tiger is no good, I tell you, put it under the microscope and shrink it, it has to be done." She opened her lips to the emetic, swallowed, gagged, gasped, and by the time they forced the rest down her throat the ambulance was pulling into the yard.

Chapter 13

They sat in Lister's office, Pruden, Madame Karitska, and Jake Bellam from the police lab. "In America," Bellam said, "thorn apple is more familiarly known as Jimson weed. It's a narcotic. The kids fool with the leaves once in a while and occasionally you hear of a death, but it's never received the publicity that LSD or marijuana have.

"The seeds," he continued, "are the *really* poisonous part of the plant, although you can get dilation of the pupils just from handling the leaves. The seeds you can boil and you can dry but nothing dilutes their poison."

He picked up the jar of instant coffee, poured some of it into his hand, and shook his head. "The other jar was only 30 per cent Jimson weed but this one—" He poured some of it into the palm of his hand. "As you can see, it's pure Jimson-weed seed. This is the one Mrs. Larkin must have made her coffee with. I see maybe a few grains of instant coffee but most of it's been replaced by the seeds."

Pruden shivered. "They look so much alike."

"Not really," Bellam said, "but when you open up a jar labeled instant coffee you assume the grains in it are coffee. There's a superficial resemblance but the instant's coffee's lighter brown. Your freeze-dried grains have the same weight, a shade chunkier perhaps, and with sharp edges instead of round. Still, to the casual glance—even to a not-so-casual glance—it would resemble coffee."

"Random killings," said Madame Karitska musingly, and lifted her glance to Pruden.

"The worst kind," Bellam said. "Aimed at no one in particular, which takes you into very deep psychological territory."

Pruden looked doubtful. "Unless a young child, a very young child—"

"Always possible," agreed Bellam. "Very young children fantasize—turn mud pies into real pies, make doll pillows out of thistledown and tea out of sugar and water. He or she could think these seeds are coffee and helpfully put them in a jar of coffee. But that's your department," he said rising. "You've rescued Mrs. Larkin in time, and you've found your poison. I'll take this jar with me, Lieutenant, have it labeled and tucked away safely for you. All I can say is—good luck."

When he had gone Pruden looked at Madame Karitska and smiled wryly. "My work is just beginning but at least they can't blame this one on Mrs. Trumbull. Any suggestions?"

"Yes," said Madame Karitska firmly. "Begin with those three young people who were sitting on the steps of the Dunlap house on Monday."

"The two Dunlaps and Joe Lister junior? I suppose one has to begin somewhere," he said thoughtfully. With a sharp glance he added, "Any particular reason?"

Her smile was dazzling. "There are always particular reasons but I am not a policeman. I find confusing threads here but perhaps you can explain them. First the motive, which is important, but there is also the astonishment to me that with this coffee so accessible there haven't been more people poisoned."

"Lister pretty much explained that," said Pruden. "He himself drinks Coke most of the time. Cas Johnson prefers tea and brings his own tea bags with him— except when he forgets. Lister says that really nobody drinks the coffee except when the Coke machine's empty." He added bitterly, "We've had unseasonably hot weather lately. The Coke machine ran out last weekend and delivery isn't due until tomorrow, and then of course there were *two* instant-coffee jars to choose from. . . ."

"Like Russian roulette," mused Madame Karitska. "Very diabolical, actually. The person who could conceive of this deliberately would have no reverence for life at all, I think, since another human being means no more than the blade of grass he or she walks on. This person would be incapable of suffering."

Pruden stared at her. *"Incapable of suffering?* What a strange way to put it! Surely mad?"

"Oh but my dear Lieutenant," she said sadly, "a human being incapable of suffering is viciously crippled. We may reject suffering but just think what we would be without it! There would be no empathy, no compassion, no remorse, and above all no growth. To have feelings so blocked, to be lacking in any sense of tragedy—" She shook her head. "What is left but hatred?"

"I'd still vote for insanity if this turns out to be premeditated murder."

"Insanity," she said, "is only a *word*."

Pruden nodded. "Okay, I'll accept that." He glanced at the clock on the wall. "School should be ending about now and in half an hour the neighborhood will be humming. I'll begin by questioning those three young people and then I'll—"

Madame Karitska gently interrupted him. "If I might make a suggestion, there is, I think, a little experiment you might perform, a little drama you might play out that could get to the heart of the matter without any waste of time. . . ."

The three sat on up-ended wooden crates just outside the rear door to the garage and regarded Pruden with varying emotions. Kathy Dunlap's eyes were eager; Birch Dunlap looked sulky but undeniably curious; and Joe Lister junior suspicious. Pruden had caught them as they descended from the school bus; their schoolbooks lay beside them.

"I asked for a few minutes of your time because I wanted to make an appeal to you three, as leaders in the neighborhood," began Pruden, and turning over an empty barrel he sat down facing them. "I've just told you what happened to Mrs. Larkin. We have no idea how she came to be poisoned, or with what she was poisoned; we only know she stood in this doorway trying to frame the word *Help,* and she had pretty much the same reactions as you did, Kathy."

"Wow," said Kathy, her eyes wide.

"So we have to conclude that the poison's somewhere in this neighborhood and we need your help."

"How, sir?" asked Birch. "You know we'll do anything we can."

"Count me in too," said Joe junior, nodding.

"And me," added Kathy.

"We need—the Coke machine's empty?" he said to Madame Karitska in surprise.

"Yes, what a pity after you gave me all those quarters," she told him. "But the water's boiling for coffee, I'll pour everyone some coffee instead. Three coffees coming up."

"Good, because we have to get down to brass tacks on this. We have to figure out a plan."

Young Joe Lister said uneasily, "Look here, you make it sound as if somebody could be going around doing this deliberately. I mean, that maybe it's not an accident?"

"Could be," said Pruden judiciously. "Could be. That's what I wanted to talk to you about." He accepted a cup of coffee from Madame Karitska's tray, added a spoonful of sugar and thanked her.

"I don't really like coffee," Kathy Dunlap said, "but if you have lots of milk it tastes like coffee ice cream."

"There's lots of milk," Madame Karitska told her, handing her the milk pitcher, and moved on to Joe Lister junior.

Joe hesitated, then reached for a cup and rejected sugar and milk.

"Birch?" said Madame Karitska.

He took a cup absently, his eyes on Pruden. "Is what Joe says possible?" he asked. "I mean, that it's murder?"

"You have here a pattern of random incidents," said Pruden, "that add up to—" He paused to watch Kathy Dunlap lift the cup to her lips and drink. "Add up to more than coincidences, maybe. First you have illnesses, and then the tragic death of— Too hot for you, Joe?" he asked.

Joe looked down at his coffee and said, "No, I was just listening to you."

"Have some."

"Sure. You mean Julie's death."

"Julie's death was rotten," Birch said angrily. "If it turns out to be a murder then I'd sure like to get my hands on—"

Pruden was staring incredulously at Joe Lister junior, who had just lifted his cup and was drinking down his coffee without hesitation. He said to Birch, "What did you say?"

"I said, if you think it's murder I'd sure like to get my hands on—"

Pruden turned to him, glanced at the cup still in his his hands and said gently, "Drink your coffee, Birch."

Birch, too, looked down at his cup and then at Pruden. "I really don't care for any, sir, I just took it to be polite."

"Drink it."

Birch looked startled. "I don't want to."

"Drink it."

Birch whitened. He said curtly, "I told you, I don't want to. I'm not going to."

Pruden moved swiftly: he took the cup from Birch's

hand and lifted it to the boy's lips, pushing his head back with one arm and holding him with the other. "I said drink it."

"No!" shouted Birch, trying to squirm beyond Pruden's reach.

Pruden held him resolutely while the others stared in astonishment. "Then tell me why you won't drink it, Birch, or I'll force it down your throat."

"Damn you," sobbed Birch. "Damn you, let me go!"

"Why, Birch, why? Drink it or tell me why."

"Because it's poison!" Birch screamed at him. "It'll kill me, that's why. Let me go, I want to go home!"

"I'll let you go," said Pruden, and turning to the others said sadly, "It isn't poisoned, of course, but he's the only one who knew it could be. Yes it was murder, Joe, and I owe you an apology; I thought if it was any of you three it would be you. Kathy, you'd better run home and get your mother now . . . in a hurry, Kathy."

On Saturday morning the Dunlap house was shuttered and silent except for Kathy Dunlap sitting on the front steps talking earnestly and tearfully with Joe Lister junior. There were no bicycle riders on Mulberry Street this weekend, or children playing hopscotch. At quarter past ten a somewhat pale Mrs. Larkin carried a tray of sandwiches through the gate of Mrs. Trumbull's house and joined a substantial number of people already inside the yard: children with grass clippers, a teenager with a power mower, and two men on ladders pruning vines away from the boarded-up windows. In the living room, from which a great number of boxes had been removed, Madame Karitska lay curled up on the couch asleep. She opened her eyes at Mrs. Larkin's arrival and sat up. "It's ten o'clock?"

"Fifteen minutes past," said Mrs. Larkin, offering her a sandwich. "Mrs. Trumbull ought to be here any minute. Lieutenant Pruden insisted we let you sleep."

"I appreciate that."

"And Lieutenant Pruden asked me to tell you that he hung a sign on your apartment door saying you'd be back at one o'clock."

"Now that really is kind," said Madame Karitska, smoothing her hair. "I'm afraid I've lost rather a lot of business these last few days."

Mrs. Larkin grinned. "Well, I'll be one of your first clients when you go back," she said. "After watching you at work yesterday and most of last night—"

"My record, alas, was very poor," sighed Madame Karitska. "It took so long—hours! I must have been very tired."

"We're all tired," said Mrs. Larkin, and abruptly sat down and put her head between her hands. "To think it was Birch, *Birch Dunlap,* of all people. Once in a while, Madame Karitska, once in a while I used to wish my two boys could be a little more like Birch. He was so self-contained, so *polite.* He never climbed trees so he could fall out of them, his clothes were always clean and tidy and his grades at school so marvelous. I used to wonder sometimes what I was doing wrong," she said, and lifted a troubled face to Madame Karitska. "He was such a *good* boy."

"Yes," said Madame Karitska.

"Is it true—did he really scream at everyone when they took him away that he wasn't sorry, that it was the first fun he'd ever had?"

"Yes," said Madame Karitska.

"My God!"

"But it would be wise to forget what he said,"
Madame Karitska pointed out gently. "He's very young,
you know, and it's to be hoped that he'll become healed
in time, and that someone may be able to teach him
how to enjoy life. It *can* be taught," she said, and then,
getting up, she added, "Do I hear a car?"

They hurried out to the porch in time to see Pruden
help Mrs. Trumbull out of his car. Her hat fell off and
he rescued it. She straightened, stared at the scene in
front of her and gasped, "People?"

Pruden grinned. "You've just discovered you're sane,
which is something not all of us know, and you're going
to have the best-groomed yard on the block. Come and
meet some of your neighbors now."

Very quietly Mrs. Trumbull began to cry. "It's just
—just that it's so terribly kind," she explained, wiping
her eyes. "but I won't be able to stay in my house."

Madame Karitska said, "You haven't told her?"

"No, I saved the big surprise until we got here." He
led her through the gate and up to the steps and suggested she sit down. Pulling a sheet of paper out of his
wallet he handed it to her. "Exhibit A, Mrs. Trumbull:
a photostat of what Madame Karitska found among
your junk early this morning. We were here all night
looking. Her good old ESP singled out the right carton
in the living room, but the problem was that what
turned out to be of value was a stamp. It was like
looking for a needle in a haystack but at four o'clock
this morning we found it."

"A stamp?" repeated Mrs. Trumbull, looking bewildered.

"I took the liberty of showing it to a dealer this

morning and then I rented a safe-deposit box for it in your name. The dealer said it's one of the rarest regular-issue United States postage stamps, only two of its kind in existence, and the other one sold at auction last year for twenty-seven thousand dollars."

"Hey, now," said Mrs. Larkin.

"Well, now," whispered Mrs. Trumbull.

"I think," said Madame Karitska gravely, "it's time to start the party. . . . Welcome home, Mrs. Trumbull."

Chapter 14

She had seen them on Eighth Street from time to time, sometimes just the woman carrying a shopping bag and looking like a cheerful little bird, and sometimes the man too, with his hand on her arm. They were a pleasing sight, for they gave every evidence of still enjoying each other's company. Their clothes were ordinary, their faces worn, but they had somehow remained uncorrupted and wholesome. They had great simplicity.

They were in fact the last two people Madame Karitska had ever expected to find at her door but—on this Thursday morning in November—here they were. They stood and looked at her and then the woman nervously cleared her throat and said, "We heard about you."

Her husband nodded and Madame Karitska noticed that his eyes were red-rimmed and swollen.

"But of course—do come in," she said. "I was about to have a cup of coffee, won't you join me?" She drew them in and closed the door.

As if he'd not heard her the man said in a harsh voice, "We wondered—we wondered, Ellen and I, if you know how to contact the dead."

"Like the seances we've seen in movies," the woman put in eagerly.

Madame Karitska's brows lifted. "I don't really approve of seances," she told them, and meeting the terrible appeal in their eyes she added, "Suppose we have some coffee and you tell me about it."

"If we could only persuade you!" cried the woman. "It's all been so sudden, it's such a shock."

"Now Ellen," said her husband.

"Please," Madame Karitska told them firmly. "Just sit down, won't you?" Walking into the kitchen she added two cups to the tray and carried it in to the low table. "You live in this neighborhood, I think, don't you?"

Each of them nodded. "Our name is Heyer, Mr. and Mrs. Fritz Heyer." The woman's hands trembled as she accepted the cup of coffee.

"We've just come from the burial," Mr. Heyer added in a broken voice.

"Try to drink a little, Fritz," his wife begged. "It's good hot coffee, just what you need."

"Our granddaughter's burial," he said.

"She's lived with us for the last ten years," explained the woman, pressing a cup of coffee into her husband's hands. "Ever since her parents died. It was like living with a songbird in the house. For ten years she was like a daughter to us—"

"She was killed in a car crash Tuesday morning on the way to the airport," broke in Mr. Heyer. "Our only son's daughter, our only grandchild. And so beautiful."

"A psychologist," put in the woman with astonishment.

"Yes, and she was on her way to the airport for her first vacation in Paris."

"I see," murmured Madame Karitska, blinking.

"It was a very bad accident. They say death must have been instantaneous, for which we're thankful—"

"—but it's frightening," said the woman, "that if it wasn't for the car's license—and the passport they found—they wouldn't even have known she was Jan. Or notified us. They might have buried her in a—in a—"

"Now, Mother," he said, patting her hand.

Madame Karitska was accustomed to being plunged into other people's worlds and she had been listening with sympathy. Now she said, "But a seance?"

"It's my wife," explained Mr. Heyer. "She can't accept it, she can't sleep, what's worst of all she can't cry. So we thought— You see, Jan had the gift of second sight—"

"Jan?"

"Our granddaughter. We never talked about it—it always alarmed us—but we thought with Jan having this second sight, as they call it, she might—well, give us a message."

"She must be waiting to give us one," put in his wife pleadingly. "Even with her own apartment now and her own friends she came to dinner with us every Sunday, and for every opera there were tickets. Always she was so thoughtful."

"But sometimes," said Madame Karitska softly, "it's better not to trouble the dead, to bind them to us. It's kinder to let them go free."

"Just one word," begged the woman. "You must understand how it was, there was only the telephone call—so abrupt, so sudden—and nothing but her effects to identify. Effects . . . such a strange word, isn't it? Because of the fire. It was so unreal."

"The fire?"

"The car began burning. She was only twenty-four, Madame Karitska, she was the light of our lives."

"Yes," said Madame Karitska and sighed. She disapproved of their request, but no matter how she personally felt she was confronted by two elderly people in need of comfort and reassurance. "I can try," she said, nodding.

"Oh bless you," cried the woman.

Madame Karitska arose and drew the curtains across the window, then asked them to move so that she could arrange three chairs in the approximation of a circle. "What was your granddaughter's full name?" she asked, sitting down.

"Jan Cooper Heyer."

She nodded, asked that they hold hands, and closed her eyes. "We are asking," she said in a low voice, "for a message from Jan Cooper Heyer, killed Tuesday in an auto accident."

There was a long silence and Madame Karitska, feeling her eyes grow heavy, knew she was slipping into a light trance. She could feel presences, she could sense disapproval, mute communications, and an uncomfortable prickling of her nerves, and then someone sneezed loudly and she opened her eyes.

It was Mr. Heyer. "I'm terribly sorry," he said. "I sneezed."

She glanced at her watch and saw that she had been in trance for nearly fifteen minutes. "Did I say anything?"

Mrs. Heyer shook her head. "Nothing."

Madame Karitska nodded. "That is the impression I gained, too. *Nothing.*"

"You'll try again?" pleaded Mrs. Heyer.

Madame Karitska tactfully skirted this by saying, "Perhaps if I had something belonging to your granddaughter it might be of some help before making another effort."

"Well—there's her passport," said Mr. Heyer doubtfully. "They gave it to me at the morgue Tuesday night and I have it with me."

"The passport that was on her when she died?"

Mr. Heyer brought it from the inside pocket of his jacket, handling it carefully, as if it were a priceless treasure. "Here," he said, pressing it into her hand.

Madame Karitska accepted it none too happily and closed her eyes over the thin blue book. The Heyers were silent, a little awed as they watched her, not understanding what this cost her, for Madame Karitska was at once plunged into the final moments of the girl's life: all other impressions faded before anything so powerful as death. The car . . . it was really quite horrible, she could feel its insane and reckless speed, she could feel the defiance and the excitement of the girl at the wheel, see her dark head bent forward, eyes narrowed, face intent, her lips moving to the beat of the music blasting from the car radio. And then came the unexpected curve in the road and the utility post leaping up in front of the windshield. She could feel the quick intake of breath, and in the split second before impact Madame Karitska experienced with Jan Heyer a glimpse into the girl's life. Then, *"Tommy!"* she screamed, and there was nothing.

Madame Karitska opened her eyes and looked at the old couple. How could she tell them that their granddaughter was not at all what they had believed her to be, that in that last moment when Jan Heyer looked into what she was and had been, Madame Karitska, too, had looked and seen her as neither kind nor good but deeply troubled and destructive.

"Yes?" asked Mr. Heyer.

"She died with the name of Tommy on her lips."

"Tommy?" They looked at each other wonderingly.

"She was too busy to go out often with men," said Mr. Heyer. "Perhaps it was one of her patients."

"Patients?"

"Yes, she was a psychologist. For a year now she's been in private practice. Two days a week she gave to the Harlow Settlement House."

"Was she a fast driver? Have you ever driven with her?"

"Many times," said Mrs. Heyer. "No, she never speeded. She was careful even about stop signs. When she was driving she wouldn't even turn on the little radio that came with the car, she said it was too distracting."

Madame Karitska said sharply, "She *was* dark-haired, wasn't she?"

"Dark!" exclaimed Mr. Heyer. "No, no, she was fair, you can see that by the passport."

Madame Karitska opened the passport and looked

at the attractive, high-cheekboned face and then she looked at them. "But this is not the young woman who was killed in the car."

"What do you mean?" faltered Mrs. Heyer.

"I mean—" Madame Karitska stopped and frowned. "I do not wish to lift your hopes, but the young woman who died in the car was dark, very restless, with much confusion in her."

"But what can you mean?" asked Mrs. Heyer in astonishment.

"I don't know," said Madame Karitska simply. "The body—the remains—were unidentifiable?"

Mrs. Heyer turned white. "Yes."

"But the passport survived?"

Mr. Heyer looked a little sick. "Yes. It was outside the car when they found her. You understand there was a fire—"

"Yes, I understand," Madame Karitska said, and nodded. "If I were you I would ask them to make further inquiries. There must be some way. Teeth, fingerprints—"

"But we just buried her," cried Mrs. Heyer. "Fritz, what is she talking about, what does she mean?"

Mr. Heyer gave Madame Karitska a reproachful look and stood up. "I think we'd better go, Mother, we've taken up too much of this lady's time."

The woman said blankly, "All right, but Fritz, I don't understand."

"She can be of no service to us, Mama," he explained gently, and helped her to her feet. Turning to Madame Karitska he said simply, "I'm sorry for you. I've heard of people like you but I thought—I'm tempted to report you to the police but we've had enough heartache. We came to you freely so I leave a dollar with you, for I'm a man who pays his debts, but to raise false hopes—this to me is the most despicable crime in the world." He spoke it like a curse.

"As you wish," said Madame Karitska. "I quite understand your feelings." She saw them to the door, closed it behind them, and glanced ruefully at the dollar he had left in the basket. For a moment she experienced doubt—enough to question herself severely, for it was very hard to be taken for a charlatan —but no, she could not doubt the impressions she'd received.

Nevertheless it was not until several appointments later that she was able to forget the searing accusations in Mr. Heyer's eyes.

That night Madame Karitska slept fitfully. She woke up at one o'clock, at two, and again at three, and found this difficult to understand because she was by custom a sound sleeper. At four o'clock she fell asleep and experienced a vivid dream. She was walking down a long hallway lined with windows. She stopped suddenly and said to the man who was escorting her—it was Pruden—"I have to look in that window."

"Why that one?" he asked.

"I don't know." She moved to the window and looked inside. Sitting on a bare cot was a young woman in blue-jeans and a faded sweat shirt. She glanced up and saw Madame Karitska and her lips silently framed two words: *Help me.*

Madame Karitska woke up and knew that the girl was Jan Heyer. It seemed a very natural dream, since the grandparents' visit was still on her mind, but on the other hand there were differences that made her thoughtful: the girl in the dream was not a copy of the photograph Madame Karitska had been shown earlier in the day. It was the same girl, yet different. Madame Karitska, for instance, remembered her from the photograph as aloof, rather like a model in a fashion magazine, with high cheekbones and a smooth blond head. In the dream the girl was not like that at all, she was almost urchin-like, her face alive and full of passion.

Pruden, stopping in early the next morning, found Madame Karitska troubled. "Something bothering you?" he asked, accepting a cup of coffee from her.

"Frankly yes, my friend. I am becoming convinced that a girl who was killed three days ago is still alive."

He said, "Perhaps you'd care to tell me about it?"

She described the Heyers' visit on the preceding day and he listened attentively. When she had finished he said, "I certainly know better than to ignore these impressions of yours, but as a detective I have to point out a few flaws in your theory that she may still be alive. For instance, if this accident took place on Tuesday—and this is Friday morning—then where *is* Jan Heyer?"

"I don't know."

"She was about to fly off on a plane to Europe. She was on her way to the airport in a car licensed and registered in her name. There was—or so we have to assume—no one else in the car with her, and it was her passport found beside the car."

Madame Karitska stirred restlessly. "Yes, yes, I know, I admit at once to you that every fact points to its being Jan Heyer who was in the car. But why, then, do I feel that she's alive?"

He looked at her so doubtfully that she laughed. "Oh, my dear Lieutenant, you wish to tell me that I am demented or, how do you say, losing the touch? This is in your mind, admit it."

His smile turned rueful. "Buddhas, not-so-innocent stepfathers, a murderess who is not a murderess—how can I believe you're demented?"

"Then help me to find her," pleaded Madame Karitska. "Prove to me that she's dead."

"Which?"

"Either."

He nodded. "It's the latter I'll have to take on, then. I can only prove to you that she's dead."

"Good," said Madame Karitska, her eyes brilliant. "And I shall try to prove to you that she's alive. Where do we begin?"

"Wait a minute," he said, "this is simple police work, double-checking all the facts."

"But the facts will not change," she pointed out. "Only their interpretation can change."

"What does that mean?"

"It means that since I am convinced that Jan Heyer was not driving the car, I must look for the young woman who *was* in the car. Could you, I wonder, secure for me a list of all the young women reported missing since Tuesday?"

Staggered, he said, "Good Lord, there must be at least fifty women reported missing since then in a city the size of Trafton."

"But there is a list, with addresses and pertinent data?"

"Oh yes."

Madame Karitska nodded. "Good. I have a 9 A.M. appointment, after which I will stop in at your headquarters and collect this list. You do not look pleased. Why?"

"You're pushing me to the wall," he said dryly, and then, responding with equal efficiency, he added, "All right, you win, I'll look into it. Suppose we meet at the Green Door Restaurant for dinner at six, and we'll compare notes." With this he put down his coffee cup, reached for his coat, and fled.

A promise was a promise, no matter how artfully wangled, thought Pruden, and after a busy morning wrapping up the threads of a burglary Pruden turned his attention to Jan Heyer, lately deceased: age twenty-four, psychologist, private office at the Community Medical Building, North Broad Street, consultant and psychologist at Harlow Settlement House. He conscientiously drove to the scene of Tuesday's accident, which had taken place just beyond the underpass on Clinton Avenue near the airport. He talked to a witness, the owner of a diner, who said the car had shot out of the underpass traveling at seventy miles an hour and skidded off the road into the utility pole.

"Not much left," the man said. "Outside the car there was a shoe and there was this passport and there were parts of a radio strewn all over the place."

"You're sure they came from the car?"

"Bloody sure. I keep my place free of litter and I'd picked the drive clean at 9 A.M. Things flew out, I could see it. A pity the girl didn't too; the car caught fire inside of a few seconds."

Pruden found the shoe still at the morgue. "We gave the passport to the old man—her grandfather, he said he was—and turned over the remains to the Jacobs Funeral Home. There didn't seem much point in giving the old man the shoe, he was in bad enough shape as it was."

It was a size-six shoe: Pruden wrote this down.

The police report was straightforward enough: the accident had yielded the charred body of a young female. The car license was H10567, a red Datsun registered in the name of Jan Heyer, 206 Boulevard, Apartment 3. Passport and left shoe found near car. Charred framework of two suitcases inside car; a sifting of ashes yielded one gold ring and the remains of a gold watch, both identified by grandfather as belonging to owner of car. Next of kin: Mr. and Mrs. Fritz Heyer, 37 Eighth Street. End of case.

There was only one more thing he could do, and after thinking about an approach to this, he telephoned the girl's grandfather. He was sorry to trouble them, he said, but a shoe had turned up at the scene of the accident and he wondered if Mr. Heyer could tell him Jan Heyer's shoe size. The old man accepted the question without curiosity. Pruden heard him call to his wife and then he came back to the telephone and said in a depressed voice, "Size seven and a half."

Pruden had expected him to say size six. It was the only piece of evidence that hadn't been checked out and he had been sorely tempted to overlook it but he was too good a policeman. This discrepancy jarred him. He said, "You're positive of this?"

"Oh yes. My wife, she has all Jan's sizes written down on a piece of paper."

It was a very *small* discrepancy, thought Pruden since everything else belonged to the girl, the car, the passport, the ring, the watch, but he realized that it had startled him. He wondered if this was because it proved to him how impervious he was to Madame Karitska's wild suggestion the girl might be alive. He thought in dismay, "I've been humoring Madame Karitska," and he wondered if she knew this.

"Yes, of course," she told him when they faced each other across a table at the Green Door Restaurant that evening. "But this is very natural under the circumstances, is it not so? I am very glad that something has made a small dent in your complacency."

"It doesn't change anything," he reminded her quickly. "The shoe could have been tossed from a passing car only moments before Jan Heyer drove out of the underpass, or a friend might have left a pair of shoes in the car."

"Yes," said Madame Karitska, regarding him with such amusement that he hastily asked her what she had learned today.

"Not much," she said. "This—how do you call it, leg work?—is very tiring. You gave me the names of twenty-one young women reported missing since Tuesday. I can tell you that Consuelo Sanchez returned home this morning, and that Nina Abbott's parents heard from her in today's mail that she has eloped and is in California." She brought the list from her purse and placed it on the table. "I have visited fifteen from the list, with four more to go. In five cases I knew at once they were wrong—they did not know how to drive, or were too old or too young—and at ten places I did readings."

"Nothing?"

"Nothing *yet*," she told him with spirit. "I shall visit the remaining four addresses after dinner."

Surprised, he said, "What about clients this evening?"

"I canceled them, this is the more important."

"Why?" he asked, staring at her curiously. "Ego? Vanity? To prove you're right?"

She gave him a steady, thoughtful glance. "It has not occurred to you, Lieutenant, that if Jan Heyer was not killed on Tuesday then wherever she is she could be in some danger?"

"No," he said calmly, "because it hasn't occurred to me yet that she wasn't killed."

"Then you have kinder dreams than I," she said shortly, and put down her coffee cup. "This has been delightful but I must go."

"I'll go with you," he said. "You shouldn't be walking all over the city alone at night."

Their third call brought them to a fourth-floor walkup on Fourth Street where the city had lately enjoyed an invasion of young people looking for low rents. The card on the door of the apartment read "Grahn and Shilhaus." A heavily made-up girl with bright red hair answered their knock.

"Is this where Carol Grahn lives?" asked Madame Karitska.

The girl looked with interest at Pruden and with undisguised indifference at Madame Karitska. "Look, she's not here and I don't know where she is. I'm not going to ask you in, I go to work in two hours—I'm a nightclub dancer—and I got to save my energy."

"Then we'll talk in the hall," said Madame Karitska.

"Is Miss Grahn a dancer too?"

"No, she floats." At the look on Madame Karitska's face the girl explained tiredly, "Floats around. Works when she needs the bread. You know, typist, stock clerk." She added quickly. "But she's trying to break into acting. Very artistic, you know? Look, who are you anyway?"

Pruden brought out his wallet and showed her his ID card. "She's been missing since Tuesday?"

"Actually since Sunday," the girl said with a shrug. "We room together—strictly a financial arrangement, you understand, you can't call us friends. Never knew her before, and we never butted into each other's affairs but we had this agreement. I mean, we found out fast that we're both nervous as hell about the city, especially at night, you know? So we made this pact that we'd sort of keep tabs on each other. If one of us didn't turn up for twenty-four hours we'd report it." She sighed. "I waited even longer, you know? *Two* nights. I kept thinking she'd show up but she didn't. I don't know, maybe she forgot our agreement but we had it and at least I kept my part of the deal."

Pruden said, "You think she'd forget something as important as that?"

"Hell, I don't know, she certainly hasn't been the same since she met Tommy; she forgets everything."

"Tommy," said Madame Karitska, suddenly alert.

"Yeah. A real clown. I don't think he's worth the time of day but she thought he was great. Me, I think he was on drugs. A crazy, hipped-up kind of guy."

Madame Karitska said hopefully, "Do you know his last name, or where we could find him?"

The girl looked tired. "Don't know a thing about him,

really I don't. No, wait a minute, I think he's the guy she met at the settlement house."

"It was Pruden who said sharply, "What settlement house?"

"Harlow. Two blocks from here. *You* know. Carol practically lived there."

"Would you," said Madame Karitska in a practical voice, "have a photograph of Carol in the apartment, or one of Tommy?"

The girl sighed. "Hell, I guess you'd better come in, it's drafty enough in this hall."

The apartment looked as if nobody had touched anything since the movers walked out. The girl rummaged in a bureau drawer, contributing further to the disorder, and drew out a piece of cardboard. "Here's her graduation picture, 1972, from Oak Falls, Nebraska. The one she had of Tommy, I've seen it, she must be carrying with her."

Madame Karitska took the picture and studied it: a girl with long dark hair, high cheekbones, laughing eyes; a young face, immature, not beautiful but eager for life. Perhaps too eager for life, thought Madame Karitska, and thanked her. "May we borrow this?"

"Be my guest."

As they descended the narrow stairs Madame Karitska said quietly, "Jan Heyer worked at the settlement house two days a week."

"I know," Pruden said grimly. "That's where we're heading next."

The Harlow Settlement House was a square, decaying brick building adjoining the old Harlow Hospital. As money had begun to flow out of Third Street in the fifties, an exodus that soon turned into a rout, the hospital and the settlement house had been left stranded, rather like middle-aged widows suddenly confronted with a vast number of children to raise and only wit and imagination to bridge the gap. Both institutions had survived, and had even acquired a kind of brash youthfulness. Life raced through their walls now like blood through an artery, pulsating, sometimes anemic, frequently needing transfusions but always managing to narrowly surmount disaster.

It was eight o'clock when they entered the building. Pruden headed first for the director's office to explain their presence to Miss Brylawski.

"Oh, it's a terrible loss," said Miss Brylawski with feeling. "Terrible. You can't replace people like Jan Heyer. The kids loved her, she talked their language. She was a darling."

"How about this girl?" asked Pruden, handing her Carol's photograph. "Her name is Carol Grahn and she spends time here. Would you know if her path ever crossed Miss Heyer's?"

"I wouldn't have the foggiest, you'll want to see Harry Jones on that," said Miss Brylawski. "You'll find him downstairs in the lion's den. Me, I sit up here doing paperwork and supplying the glue that holds the place together."

Harry Jones proved easy to find: he was huge and black and he looked as if he could supply considerable glue to hold things together too. His glance assessed both Madame Karitska and Pruden before he said amiably, "Sure, I know Carol. Used to hang around with Tommy Brudenhall."

"Ah," said Madame Karitska triumphantly.

"Used to?" repeated Pruden.

"Haven't seen Carol since Tommy split. He worked here—janitor work. We gave him a room in the basement. Sunday he just left."

"What's his background?" asked Pruden, and meeting that level stare again he sighed and brought out his wallet. "Police," he explained.

"I see." The eyes didn't waver. "Miss Brylawski clear this?"

"We stopped there first. She knows me."

"Okay, then. Tommy had a police record, he'd been in prison. We try to give a break to kids like that."

"Do you know whether Carol was ever a patient of Jan Heyer's?" asked Madame Karitska.

His eyes flickered. "That girl's death cost me something, man. One hell of a sweet kid, Jan. Just out of school, you know? Really with it."

Madame Karitska tactfully asked her question again.

"Patient? I wouldn't know, but Chick or Deirdre would. They saw Jan regularly, and the kids with regular appointments always seemed to know who else went. Like a club." He pointed to a door down the corridor. "You go in there—that's my office—and I'll send along anybody I can find. We're having basketball play-offs, there should be someone."

Actually Harry found several young people who had been patients of Miss Heyer when she visited the settlement house. Chick's appointments were on Wednesday, and he said he'd never seen Carol Grahn leaving the office or waiting to go in. Miranda knew Carol but had no idea whether she had ever had therapy with Jan Heyer. Then Deirdre bounced into the office, eager, joyous, and winsome. Deirdre was sixteen, with a fine-

boned black face and a smile as brilliant as a sunrise.
Yes, Carol had visited Miss Heyer twice as a patient,
she reported, because Carol had told her so. Carol
had hated the psychologist after seeing her, because
Miss Heyer had suggested that she come in regularly
for help, and Carol hadn't liked that at all. It was,
Deirdre announced with authority, a typical love-hate
relationship because although Carol hated the psychologist she imitated her too. Like the wig, for instance.

"Wig?" said Madame Karitska quickly.

"It was about a week ago," explained Deirdre. "I
had a Saturday-morning appointment with Miss Heyer,
nine o'clock, and the door to her office was open so
I walked in and Miss Heyer was standing with her back
to me looking out the window. On Saturdays, you see,
she often came in wearing blue jeans—it was on week-
days she always wore suits and stuff—so I really
thought it was Miss Heyer. Then she turned around and
it was Carol, wearing a blond wig. She looked so much
like Miss Heyer I couldn't believe my eyes."

"Wig," repeated Pruden, and for the first time felt
that kindling of excitement that came to him when a
piece of unexpected information gave a new dimension to a case. "Go on."

"Carol laughed and said she was playing a joke on
Miss Heyer. She pulled off the wig and put it in a little
box and told me not to tell or I'd spoil things. Then
she went out."

"What did you think of Carol?" asked Madame
Karitska softly.

Deirdre considered this a moment before saying
earnestly, "Nice, but really heavy dependency needs.
We played ping-pong a lot but if any man came along

she'd switch right away and put on a big act. Very juvenile," Deirdre explained scornfully. "You'd never guess she was twenty, she was more like sixteen or seventeen inside, and Tommy wasn't good enough for her at *all,* but she wanted somebody and it didn't matter much who."

"Thanks, Deirdre," Pruden said. "Thanks very much." When she had gone he looked at Madame Karitska and nodded. "I think I've got enough to order an exhumation now. I think it's time we find out once and for all who's buried in Jan Heyer's grave."

In the morning the Saturday edition of the Trafton *Times* carried the photographs of Jan Heyer and Carol Grahn with the caption: HAS ANYONE SEEN THESE WOMEN SINCE TUESDAY? As usual the newspaper had no sooner reached the stands than the telephone calls began, all of them needing to be sifted, tirelessly examined for the single piece of information that might yield a clue or a motive to this possible confusion of identities, and then at eleven o'clock Detective-Sergeant Michelangelo walked into Pruden's office and handed him a motive on a silver platter.

He said, "I don't know if you remember me, Lieutenant, I worked out of the Dell precinct and I recently handled all your inquiries about John Tortorelli?"

"Of course," said Pruden, shaking his hand. "What can I do for you, Sergeant?"

Michelangelo began talking, and before he had even finished his story Pruden interrupted him to call Madame Karitska, ordered a patrol car sent for her, and asked the Chief and Swope to come to his office. They were waiting for him when Michelangelo left, and

Pruden, ushering the three into his office, understood that his moment of truth had arrived. Swope had met Madame Karitska at the hospital, had in fact held several conversations with her on the subject of psychic phenomena, but the Chief knew nothing about her. The Chief was also a man who demanded proofs of every fact presented to him and barely tolerated intuition; the introduction of a psychic into the case could prove stormy.

He said bluntly, "Madame Karitska is a clairvoyant who's helped me on a number of cases. I called her in because she was the first—in fact the *only*—person to believe that Jan Heyer may still be alive."

The Chief blinked. He gave Madame Karitska a startled glance but made no comment, only saying impatiently, "We won't know until after the exhumation whether Miss Heyer's alive. I take it you've discovered something new since last night?"

"A motive," said Pruden, holding up a photograph. "A reason why Carol Grahn could have masqueraded as Jan Heyer. Sergeant Michelangelo brought this to my office a few minutes ago. You know we've had a communication lag because of the teletype strike, but this is a blown-up photo of the young woman who robbed the Trafton National Bank on Tuesday morning. At 9 A.M.," he emphasized, and placed the photograph on the desk in front of them.

Madame Karitska examined it first before handing it to the Chief. "A surprisingly clear photograph," she said.

Pruden nodded. "Obviously an amateur or she would have known where the bank's surveillance camera was concealed."

The Chief said, "It looks a hell of a lot like the Grahn girl. Damn it, it *is* the Grahn girl."

"I think so too," said Pruden. "What's more, Tommy Brudenhall's police record came in after I talked to you last night. He was convicted of armed robbery of a bank. If you put the two facts together——"

Swope whistled. "It makes a picture, Lieutenant."

"Okay, how do you figure it?" the Chief demanded.

Pruden said quietly, "I've begun to think Madame Karitska's right, and that Carol Grahn was driving the Heyer car when it crashed on Tuesday. Everyone at the settlement house knew about Miss Heyer's upcoming trip abroad. It was her first, and she was excited. Maybe Carol commented to Tommy that some people had all the luck, and it gave Tommy the idea, or perhaps they'd been planning a bank job to get their hands on some money and here was the perfect getaway scheme: Carol, with the same height and build as Jan Heyer, same shape of face, same high cheekbones. The difference in hair could be easily solved by a blond wig and she'd look enough like Jan Heyer to get through passport controls. They'd split the money before she left—they netted sixty thousand dollars in the robbery—and Tommy would join her in another country later.

"Jan Heyer's plane was due to leave at 12:30 P.M.," he continued. "I think they planned the robbery for 9 A.M., with Tommy outside in a car, and I'd guess that by then they'd already hijacked Jan Heyer's car and luggage, and probably Jan Heyer as well. After the bank holdup Carol changed into Miss Heyer's clothes and set out for the airport in her car, with her luggage, passport, wallet, and other identification."

"And was killed," concluded Swope.

They were silent and then the Chief said, "In that case where is Jan Heyer?"

Pruden said grimly, "My guess is that she was stashed away somewhere on Monday night by Tommy and Carol, and now only Tommy Brudenhall knows where she is, and if he buys newspapers he may be in California by this time."

"Good Lord," said the Chief. "And no way to find her?"

"I think," Madame Karitska said calmly, "that I may be of some help to you here."

Until now the Chief had successfully avoided acknowledging her presence; grudgingly he turned to look at her, saying coldly, "Oh?"

"I dreamed of Jan Heyer again last night," she said, addressing herself to Pruden exclusively. "She was in a small room, this time with no windows, the walls of rough board, and in the room there was a broken-down bed to which she was handcuffed. There were burlap sacks in one corner, and on the wall a yellowed picture of your President Roosevelt. She was quite alone.

"I want to say at once," she added firmly, "that this was no ordinary dream. Jan Heyer's grandparents mentioned to me that Jan possessed 'second sight,' which is an old-fashioned expression meaning that a person has psychic capabilities or," she said with a thoughtful glance at the Chief, "some degree of clairvoyance. I believe that in both my dreams—last night's in particular—I was in telepathic communication with Miss Heyer."

The Chief began to look distinctly uneasy. Pruden, with a glance at him, grinned and said, "Try to keep in mind, Chief, that it's Madame Karitska who's insisted all along that Jan Heyer wasn't killed."

"I'll try but it's not easy," growled the Chief.

Swope, less traumatized by this jump into the unknown, said, "But Trafton's a large city; that room you described could be anywhere."

"It might be possible," suggested Madame Karitska, "to establish more closely the area in which she's been hidden. I feel that Jan Heyer must have some experience in telepathic sending, or that this very charged emotional situation—her desperation, perhaps—has brought it to her. It is a situation very unusual, this, but it has great potential. Obviously she is a sender. Whether she can also receive telepathically, I do not know."

"You make it sound like two-way radio," said the Chief accusingly.

She smiled. "I only wish it were so easy! If you would like me to attempt some communication as an experiment, I would suggest calling in Mr. Faber-Jones and Gavin O'Connell to help."

"What else would you need?" asked Swope curiously.

"A room in which we could sit very quietly, preferably in the dark, and become receptive to what she may be projecting. But I am thinking also that it might be possible, with the three of us working, to send her the impression that we are listening, and ask her if she can in any way project a picture of where she is. This will take time. It will also be very tiring, but the three of us can work in shifts."

"Weird," said the Chief flatly, and then, "Any chance of this working?"

"You might consider the alternatives," Pruden

pointed out. "At the moment they register zero."

"True," the Chief said, turning thoughtful, and they waited, watching him. He said at last, "All right, we'll try it, we've nothing to lose but our reputations. Pruden, get the lady what she needs." He rose, looked down at Madame Karitska, started to speak, and then thought better of it and walked out.

Because it was Saturday, Gavin was summoned from St. Bonaventure's without the necessity for taxing explanations. Mr. Faber-Jones was discovered at home lunching, and agreed to collect Gavin on his way to headquarters. They arrived, curious and interested.

"This is the girl," Madame Karitska said, showing them the photograph in the *Times* after she had explained the circumstances. "She probably has no idea that she's believed dead, but she would know she is missing and that her grandparents would be worried. I think she has been trying very hard to reassure them telepathically, but with no success. Or perhaps," said Madame Karitska thoughtfully, "she did meet with some success, because they felt uneasy enough to think of a seance. Through them she was, in a sense, introduced to me."

"And walked into your dreams," Gavin said, nodding.

"Yes, but it is relatively easy to receive telepathic communication in dreams; it happens frequently to most people without their realizing it. What we must attempt here is a deliberate communication in a waking state."

"How?" asked Gavin eagerly.

"It would be not so different from your turning of

the pages in a book, Gavin . . . To send a message, at least. You would empty the mind of thought and bring attention—attention like a laser beam—on any message we send to Miss Heyer. To receive a message telepathically requires a technique similar to meditation: an emptying of the mind, stillness, and total passiveness. Also patience," she added wryly.

Faber-Jones looked doubtful. "Are you sure you want me? I'm so damned new at this and frankly it still strikes me as ridiculous, even though I've felt these things happen."

"My friend, we need your confidence and your strength," she said warmly. "Please, do not be doubtful. I suggest we start by projecting a picture of ourselves seated in those three chairs, waiting to learn where she is. If she can just *feel* our attention, it may give her support."

"I'm ready," Gavin told her.

Faber-Jones nodded.

"Good," said Madame Karitska. "I think we do this as a team for fifteen minutes—perhaps a small light under the clock will not distract us—and then you, Gavin, take a break for fifteen minutes, then Faber-Jones will rest, after which I will take fifteen minutes. Is this agreeable?"

Pruden found a small desk lamp in a nearby office and set it up in a corner. The overhead lights were turned off, the one window shuttered and the telephone disconnected. He left them in semidarkness, seated quietly in a row in the center of the room, and just to be certain they wouldn't be interrupted he posted Benson down the hall to guard the room from intruders. He noticed as he left that it was just one o'clock.

By two o'clock there had been one hundred and twenty telephone calls in answer to the photographs in the *Times,* and every available policeman was at work checking out the leads. Making it even more intricate was the fact that Tommy Brudenhall's description had been included in the *Times* article; Pruden divided his men into three groups. In the meantime the exhumation had taken place and Jan Heyer's dental charts were being traced. Her dentist turned out to be a Daniel Murk, D.D.S., with a Broad Street address. It was difficult finding him, but by half past two it was determined without any further doubt that the girl killed in the accident was not Jan Heyer. A man was detailed to notify the elder Heyers of this, and Pruden made his way up to the third floor to see if anything was happening there. He found Gavin sipping a glass of milk in the hall with Benson. "Well?" he asked somewhat curtly, the incongruity and the hopelessness of this sweeping over him.

"Nothing *really,*" Gavin said. "We're going to stop sending and begin receiving when I go back. We're all getting awfully tired."

"What do you mean, nothing *really?*"

"Jonesy had the feeling once—it scared him, though, and he panicked—of making contact with something. Or somebody, I mean. It's too bad he panicked, although I guess I would have too," Gavin said modestly. "He said it was like walking into somebody's mind for a second. It must have been spooky."

Pruden said curiously, "Did he think it was hers?"

Gavin sighed. "He hopes not. He said there was an awful kind of despair—hopelessness, actually—and a physical sensation of cold and thirst. It wasn't so good."

"Cold," repeated Pruden and then he said, "Oh God, the cold, I hadn't thought of that."

"I'd better go in now," said Gavin and handing his empty glass to Benson he tiptoed back inside.

At three o'clock the owner of a delicatessen on River Avenue called in to report that a young man resembling Tommy Brudenhall had bought five sandwiches at his shop on Tuesday night. His description of the young man matched Tommy closely enough to be promising, and Pruden ordered patrolmen to concentrate on River Avenue and begin checking out buildings in that area. At best it would be like searching for a needle in a haystack: the area was honeycombed with old warehouses, two freight stations, wharves, and abandoned buildings.

And then at quarter past five Benson paged him from an office telephone and asked him to come upstairs. He sounded excited. "They say they've got something."

Pruden raced upstairs and found the three psychics talking in the hall. Madame Karitska said eagerly, "We all received it—all of us, simultaneously. It was marvelously clear and strong. It has to mean something: a glass of beer."

"A *what?*" said Pruden blankly.

"A glass of beer. Amber liquid with white foam in a glass mug."

Pruden tried not to show his disappointment. "You really think it's important?"

Faber-Jones said stiffly, "My dear Lieutenant, you can't expect a full-blown telegram; of course it has to mean something. Just the *sending* of such a picture took enormous concentration. Enormous."

"Beer," Pruden repeated. "Beer . . . malt . . . foam

. . . a glass mug . . . Cocktail bar, maybe? Saloon?" Then he gasped, *"Brewery!* The old Wirlitzer place is down there near Convention Hall." He snapped his fingers. "Benson, send a message—oh, to hell with it, come on, let's go."

When the car pulled up in front of the huge, dilapidated old Wirlitzer Building it was six o'clock and the first flakes of snow had begun to drift through the circles of light carved out of the darkness by the street lamps. A cold November wind blew in from the river, setting Pruden's teeth on edge. Even when he turned off the siren there was no cessation of sound as other patrol cars converged on the scene, their headlights invading the black silhouette of the building. Pruden climbed out of his car to meet the others and they conferred quietly near the boarded-up entrance to the brewery.

"Can we go too?" asked Gavin when Pruden returned to the car.

"Not on your life," Pruden told him. "That place was condemned eight years ago. There's also no way of knowing whether Tommy Brudenhall's in there, armed. If it *is* the right place," he added, with a worried glance at the sky.

"We just have to wait?" Gavin asked, disappointed.

"We just have to wait," Pruden told him, and began unwinding his walkie-talkie.

Occasionally Swope's voice drifted in to them, reporting the top floor searched, and then the second floor, and once or twice they could see the flash of lights moving behind shuttered windows. The snow blurred and softened the harsh outlines of the building and danced through the beams of the spotlights set up to illuminate the door. Nobody spoke.

Suddenly Swope's voice interrupted the appalling silence. "We've found her!" he shouted. "We've found her, Lieutenant! Down in the basement."

Gavin reached out and touched Madame Karitska, found her hand and squeezed it.

"But you'd better call an ambulance," added Swope. "She's pretty weak. Says Brudenhall hasn't been around for three days. No food, no water. As soon as we get the handcuffs off her we'll be up."

They climbed out of the car and stood waiting in the howling wind, the snowflakes biting their eyes. Presently the wooden door opened slowly. Pruden went forward to help, followed at a distance by the others, so that he was the first to see her as she moved into the spotlight. She didn't look at all like her passport picture, he thought. She limped toward him supported by two policemen, tall and loose-limbed, looking younger than he'd expected in a pair of old blue-jeans and a dirty sweat shirt, long, pale-gold hair framing a gamin face.

He said with a sense of awe, "Hello there."

"She wants to meet the Karitska woman," said Benson.

Jan Heyer broke away and stumbled toward Madame Karitska, half laughing, half crying. "Meet?" she said, embracing her. "But I already know you—know you all so well!"

Pruden watched her turn toward Faber-Jones and Gavin, and he felt an inexplicable stab of jealousy. The ambulance attendant moved forward to help and Pruden, oddly reluctant to see her go, walked to the door of the ambulance and waited there.

The girl passed him. Seeing him in the spotlight for the first time she gave him a startled glance and said, *"Oh!"* and then added shyly, "Thank you very much." The doors closed behind her, the driver climbed inside, and the ambulance pulled away, leaving him standing there alone.

"Well, my friend?" said Madame Karitska, joining him.

He said in astonishment, "She's lovely."

"Yes, and so fair-haired," pointed out Madame Karitska, her eyes mischievous.

"But, damn it," he said helplessly, "all I could say was 'hello there.' She'd been through hell and all I could do was gape at her like a bloody schoolboy and say 'hello there.'"

"Yes," said Madame Karitska, amused. "Nevertheless you will see her again. Would you have preferred to throw your coat on the ground for her to walk on? It would have become very wet, my friend, for I doubt that you've noticed but it's snowing quite hard now."

"You don't understand," Pruden said angrily. "I felt such a clumsy fool . . . I feel like such a fool *now*."

Madame Karitska regarded him with impatience. "My dear Lieutenant," she said, "if you could only turn the kaleidoscope a fraction of an inch the view would dazzle you! In the meantime, however, it is excruciatingly cold here and Gavin has begun sneezing and what we all need is a cup of very hot strong coffee —Turkish, of course. Shall we go?"